The Handyman

The Handyman

A NOVEL

Carolyn See

RANDOM HOUSE   NEW YORK

LIBRARY OF CONGRESS CATALOGING-IN-PUBLICATION DATA

SEE, CAROLYN.
     THE HANDYMAN / CAROLYN SEE. — 1ST ED.
          P.   CM.
     ISBN 0-375-50155-X (ACID-FREE PAPER)
     I. TITLE.
   PS3569.E33H36   1999
   813'.54—DC21   98-21098

PRINTED IN THE UNITED STATES OF AMERICA ON ACID-FREE PAPER

RANDOM HOUSE WEBSITE ADDRESS: WWW.ATRANDOM.COM

FIRST EDITION

9   8   7   6   5   4   3   2

BOOK DESIGN BY BARBARA M. BACHMAN

for Robert Laws

my bon vivant

brother

JOHN SIMON GUGGENHEIM
MEMORIAL FOUNDATION
90 PARK AVENUE
NEW YORK, NEW YORK 10016

GUGGENHEIM APPLICATION
STATEMENT OF PLAN
August 15, 2027

ROBERT HAMPTON Y LOS TESTIGOS

BY PETER LAUE

My "plan," if I should receive this grant, is to trace imag-
istic connections between the very earliest work of Robert
Hampton (eight surviving paintings, as well as a small
collection of wooden animals, all owned by the self-
proclaimed "Testigos" or "Witnesses"), and a large body of
his intermediate work, most of which has been kept off the
market and is currently stored at his main compound between Cuernavaca and Mexico City.

In 2025 and 2026 I was able to travel to Los Angeles,
Lausanne, and the south of France to track down and
interview the original "Testigos." My work on them has
been accepted by Art of the Americas and will be published
in November of this year. Since this material is not yet
in print, however, I will be quoting from it here fairly
extensively.

I have also been fortunate enough to have received a
grant from the Lannon Foundation, which allowed me to

journey, in January of this year, to the Hampton Compound. During the two weeks of my stay I was allowed access to many of the stored paintings, and was also able to secure an invitation to return for a year to continue my work. A Guggenheim grant would cover my travel and living expenses during that time.

I feel confident that no other scholar has approached Hampton's work from this point of view. Most criticism has either concerned itself with his vast museum pieces (and has been, as a consequence, heavily theoretical) or has dealt only with Los Testigos and the rest of the Hampton myth in purely biographical terms. I would hope that a year of close research may combine the two approaches and yield up the first authentic, significant Hampton scholarship.

My "Statement" will be divided into three parts: (I) A few words on Robert Hampton, his career up to this point, and the criticism it has so far generated; (II) A short account of "Los Testigos," the surviving artworks in their possession, and the position the artist holds within this band of early acquaintances; (III) A very brief summation of what I was able to find during my stay at the compound.

I. THE ARTIST

By the year 2015, Robert Hampton had been acknowledged by most European critics to be perhaps the preeminent international artist of the new century. By most accounts, he had been among the first to cast off the debilitating angst of the twentieth century, and the ever more sterile conceptual art that had become the emblem of its anomie and affectlessness, so popular then, so dated now.

He is rightly said to be obsessed by light, color, and space. Along with this facile Renaissance comparison, he is often ranked with Renoir, Manet, and Monet, though scarcely ever said to be in their debt. Indeed, he has been more often mentioned in the same context as Latin literary figures from the century's turn, such as Gabriel García Márquez and Tomás Eloy Martínez.

I believe—though many of my colleagues might disagree—that the artist precedes the critic: The language with which to properly assess Robert Hampton's work does not yet exist. In my view, most contemporary critics have attempted to define his techniques, his world view, in the stunned, barbaric idiom with which the first astronauts described the moon. Second, for reasons that, frankly, still remain unclear to me, Hampton has so far been revered—venerated, even—quite as much for his life, his "myth," as for his work.

Hampton presently makes his home in the inviting countryside between Mexico City and Cuernavaca. (He also keeps a studio in a small town near the southern tip of the Baja California peninsula.) His home outside the capital is, as I have said, a spacious compound, where he lives with his wife and his three children, Valerie, Samantha, and Benjamin. His stepson, Teodoro M. L. Hampton, has long kept a guest house on the property, and together with his mother, manages the day-to-day workings of the artist's enterprise. It was Teodoro's idea to open the grounds once a month as early as 2015, so that both serious students and the general public could ponder the connections between art and life so essential to the development of this artist's vision. Hampton has been rigorously schooled, his stepson likes to say, in all the techniques of the previous century, and even studied (for a very short time) at the École des Beaux-Arts in Paris. But he turned his back on all that, and cast his lot with the new world and the new century.

The family makes no attempt to hide or close itself off: Visitors often glimpse Valerie and Samantha playing tennis; Ben frequently drops by with friends. There are always picnics and parties somewhere on the grounds. Teodoro Hampton, dazzlingly handsome and endlessly courteous, never tires of pointing his siblings out to the pilgrims, reminding them that these young adults were once the models for the "golden" children whom Hampton has painted through the years. He himself, Teodoro reminds them, appeared in Twilight, The Pool Series, Cabo, La Bufadora, and many other early works.

Often, the artist joins his stepson. Hampton moves among the crowd, shaking hands—a slight, tanned man, wiry, with close-cropped graying hair, and sometimes the whimsical conceit of a bolo tie fastened with turquoise. He resembles nothing so much as an American family man, and, of course, he is that. (His own mother resides on the property, but is seldom seen.) He states repeatedly that he owes a great deal, everything, to his wife.

People speculate ceaselessly about Señora Hampton, who has long been considered one of Mexico City's great beauties. In public, she dresses simply, her slim arms heavy with the gold jewelry her husband makes for her. She seems to many to be deceptively "ordinary" in her behavior, the very picture of open American friendliness. But in financial negotiations regarding her husband's work, Mrs. Hampton has been notoriously astute. With the help of her assistant and Hampton archivist, Barbara MacKenzie (whom Hampton met years ago at Otis Art Institute in

Los Angeles), Señora Hampton speedily amassed the artist's fortune. She was quick to realize the monetary value in his work, to see that the thirst consumers developed for it corresponded directly to its scarcity. By keeping at least half his work off the market she has made her husband a very rich man. There are even tales that she accomplished this at first against his will—that he would have been content to live quietly as an artisan fashioning tourist "rubbish" on the Baja coast. But when one is in the presence of those vast canvases, which sing with color and energy, one discards that story as apocryphal.

Hampton's early, smaller, more accessible work is still most beloved by the general public. When pilgrims visit the Hampton Compound or any of the major museums, they are most apt to leave with reproductions of some of his twenty-four interpretations of The Junction Between Earth and Sky, all 36″ × 44″, all filled to bursting with color and detail. In technique they have sometimes been compared to Le Douanier Rousseau, but these comparisons are specious. Rousseau's world is closed and dreamy; the light that pours from Hampton's canvases is tropical, searing, totally untamed.

Much has been written about Hampton's secular saints in The Junction series—the dying boy watched over by an ardent lover or devoted father; the anti-virgin, or Lilith, a woman who compels desire even as she admits to, flaunts, her age. And of course the exquisite, water-soaked families painted in hot light and cool blue gardens, who incontrovertibly live in another world, but where? These worlds confound the viewer. Part of Hampton's appeal has always been that his vision is often literally inexplicable: as I have suggested, the critical vocabulary has not yet been invented, the terms not coined, that explain and define his work.

But it is my contention that these twenty-four paintings boast an even earlier provenance: eight primitive
prototypes; The Child and His Guardian, The Child Assumpted into Heaven, The Guardian Alone, The Aging
Lilith, five floral still lifes (and, of course, The Animals).
All currently owned by "Los Testigos," the Witnesses.

II. Los Testigos

In Los Angeles a zealous group of disciples—self-styled
"Testigos" or Witnesses—insist they knew the artist in his
youth, and they speak of him as a man of both saintly
modesty and fierce passion. They turn up again and again,
in interviews on public television, in Sunday supplements,
even in learned journals. This group has little in common
except that they all claim to have known Hampton in his
youth, at the turn of the century.

Jamé Hareh-Tran runs an animal sanctuary in the bar-
ren canyons to the north of Los Angeles. She recalls Hampton as a spiritual healer and natural lover of children, a
man who, merely by coming into a room, banished the sor-
rows of the abandoned and the lonely: "My children loved
him. He was wonderful with my animals. I myself adored
him beyond words." Mrs. Tran has in her possession six
unique and probably genuine wooden Hamptons—two
monkeys, a snake, a bird, a turkey, and an iguana rendered in his distinctive signature green, the theological
color of hope. She has mounted these artifacts in tem-
perature-controlled, museum-quality frames in the receiv-
ing room of her wildlife refuge.

Other Testigos revere him as well. Henry William Hurst
owns three prototype acrylics of what he calls The Child

Jesus at the Junction of Good and Evil. He also claims to
be the original "Guardian Lover" above the dying Savior
with the caste mark. It's difficult to associate the graying,
distinguished public-health activist with the fervent "Guardian," but Hurst's argument is unequivocally backed by
these intriguing originals that unmistakably bear the
magic signs of the early Hampton. Hurst's longtime com-
panion, Alec Austen, also claims to have known the artist.

Two other prominent Californians knew Hampton at
that time. David and Shelley (Ross) Baxter were both acquainted with him during a fateful summer, and—like
Hurst and Austen—claim to have met each other through
the good offices of the artist. "We were all in our twenties,"
Baxter says. "He's the one who introduced me to Shelley.
He helped her that summer, when she was at loose ends."

It's difficult to think of investment banker Shelley Baxter as ever having been "at loose ends." Mrs. Baxter has
served on many boards, including that of the San Diego
Museum of Modern Art. (It was through her personal ef-
forts that the museum was able to acquire the Hampton
Paradise Lost and Found triptych, which claims its own
room at that site.) Her husband, a respected urban planner, claims to have been influenced by Hampton at a critical "junction" in his own life. "When we conceive of
communities, we often get caught up in our own inven-
tiveness, in an aesthetic that puts the 'plan' before the individual. Put another way, we philosophize ourselves to
death. We give people what they should need instead of
what they love. Hampton knows—always did know—that
people crave air, gardens, animals, children. My communities make room for all these elements."

The Baxter home boasts five contemporary Hamptons—

floral masterpieces in lavender, yellow, morning-glory blue, a bamboo piece in his signature green, and a slightly later hyperreal Nasturtium Study in dark orange. More significantly for this study, they also own four prototypes of these large works, hung in a small den and generally kept from public view.

The Baxters maintain their friendship with the Hamptons, seeing them several times a year, as does Valerie Le Clerc, reputed inspiration for the Lilith series. An elderly lady of great dignity and rectitude, she resides in the Hollywood Hills home she has owned for decades. (Her dearest friend for many years has been Laura Huxley, widow of the legendary Aldous Huxley, and Madame Le Clerc has said that if she herself has ever made any "contribution" to the larger world, it is because of Huxley and Hampton.) "Many of us strive and strive for nothing," she says. "That was the essential mark of the last century, and I believe it was a source of the pervasive discontent of that time. When I first met Robert, I was struck by his utter lack of striving, his absolute reluctance to claim his own greatness. To know him was to love him."

"Love" him? Can it be that Valerie Le Clerc was the original Lilith? When asked this, Madame Le Clerc laughs. "Get out your calendar," she says. "I was close to sixty in 1996." Still, an astonishing early Lilith hangs in her bedroom, so disturbing in its eroticism that the observer—however worldly—blushes to see it.

Perhaps the most unexpected of all "The Witnesses" is June Shaw, controversial professor of gender philosophy at the University of Lausanne. "Robert Hampton and I were lovers at the turn of the century," she claims. "Before we formed our attachment, he could have easily been dismissed as a loose construct of erroneous assumptions and badly thought-out premises. He was an idiot savant, if you will, utterly unconscious of himself and the world in which he lived. Our coupling changed all that. I brought him to an understanding of carnal knowledge. I am Lilith—as is any woman who dares to make that desperate choice." Absolutely nothing in Professor Shaw's physical appearance ties her to Lilith, and there is no corroborating evidence that she was ever Hampton's mistress and muse. But there can be no denying that June Shaw may have, more than any other American critic or scholar, contributed to Hampton's early artistic reputation, insisting upon his greatness and on her own contribution to it. (And it was she, in an early monograph in 2009, who coined the term "Testigos," also insisting upon the Iberianization of the word.)

Are there other Testigos? Only one woman of legendary charm—much married—who has drifted from California to the south of France for close to three decades. Some years ago, thanks to a postdoctoral grant, I was able to track down "Kate" in the town of La Ciotat on the Mediterranean coast; that preliminary interview, in fact, has led to my lifelong preoccupation with Los Testigos. Kate is an attractive, ample woman, very much a "Hampton beauty." Her diffidence, too, is Hamptonesque. "I'm not even sure he's the person you're looking for," she told me, "Or that I am. I can't believe he's 'the Robert Hampton.' For one thing—I think we were lovers once, but I hardly remember it. And wouldn't I remember it? I can tell you one thing. The boy I remember was dear. To me that counts for more than being a great lover or a great artist." She laughed, and added, "Maybe that's why I've been married so often. Maybe I'm still looking for a man like Bob."

As I stated before, I was able to spend two weeks during January of this year at the Hampton Compound. Señora Hampton was enjoying a visit from her married stepdaughter, and several students from around the world were beginning a season of "color fellowships" under Hampton's supervision and the more direct tutelage of Teodoro M. L. Hampton. With the artist's permission, I was able to spend many hours in the large studios where the artist stores his completed, intermediate works. Once again, I was struck by the fusion of the ordinary and the divine—the "sacredness" of Lilith, the transcendent quality of his floral still lifes, the inexorable insistence upon the infinite within the quotidian. Even in this cursory search I was able to find dozens of paintings that hewed to the themes of the Testigo works—the dying boy with his devoted guardian; the same boy assumpted above city crowds; the pagan woman, nude, again and again, assuming the posture and demeanor of a saint. It's often been said that Hampton is a "visionary"; from the evidence of these paintings I would argue that he has perhaps always been a Christian mystic in his own world view, obsessed with the miraculous, the divine.

Independent of the Testigo themes, I also found numerous depictions of women and girls, plainly dressed, walking in air, walking on water. And I was struck in particular by another pair of "saints" who turned up repeatedly and are plainly from the same early and intermediate periods; men who resemble Saints Peter and Paul but are dressed as American peasants, dreamy men, benign of visage, invariably presented against a celestial silver background. Threads of ineffable fire spurt from their fingernails, as miracles—dare we speculate?—waiting to occur.

When I asked the artist about these representations, he said only that he was glad I had discovered them, and that, yes, they did carry great significance. To be truthful, Hampton was less than forthcoming about his work. At times, I believe, he found my questions amusing.

Soon after that first interview, we were called to dinner, a family dinner like so many others at the compound, with its commanding view of the valley descending toward Cuernavaca. Tables had been set up under awnings outside, by a brook and waterfall of the artist's own construction. Lanterns were lit in the twilight; exotic Hampton "animals," birds and reptiles elegantly lit, could be glimpsed in the surrounding trees. A few small children romped on the lawn as the adults conversed. Robert Hampton ate with a good appetite; his wife—her arm about the waist of her visiting stepdaughter—remained standing until she was sure the party was served.

I admit that at first I was too shy to join the others. I kept to myself out on the darkening lawn, envying all of them in their easy pleasure. But Robert Hampton looked up and saw me in the dark. He got up from the table, came and took me by the arm. I was a lonely scholar, an outsider, no longer. A grant, of course, would allow me to pursue all this much further.

Peter Laue

PETER LAUE
LOS ANGELES,
MEXICO CITY
AUGUST 15, 2027

The Handyman

Part One

C H A P T E R

1

In May of 1996 I flew to Paris from Los Angeles, to get settled in the city before I enrolled in the fall semester of the École des Beaux-Arts. I was twenty-eight years old; I had a bachelor's degree in Fine Arts from UCLA and ten thousand dollars in traveler's checks. I'd spent one summer in Paris before, when I was eighteen. I'd been out of school for five years, "finding myself"—thinking I might be an artist—but that search had turned up nothing. In Paris, at least, I had the idea that I could see what others had done, and what I might do. I was scared shitless.

My plane landed at Orly at quarter of six on a cold Tuesday morning. I had a long wait for my luggage, since I'd brought enough in theory to live for a year, and I had a hard and embarrassing discussion with a cab driver when I finally got out of the airport. I'd expected to feel great, but the jet lag—maybe—kept me from being happy as the taxi drove through suburbs and grimy fog.

I had to keep reminding myself that a lot of other artists had come to this city. All of them must have had a first day, and that day had to have been lonesome.

I kept waiting for the city to turn into something beautiful, but I had a fair wait. After about forty minutes, we came in sight of the river, and yes, everything was as great as everyone said. I gave the driver the address of the Hôtel du Danube on the rue Jacob, on the Left Bank. It was too expensive for me but I'd allowed myself a week there, since it was close to the École, the Musée d'Orsay, the Louvre, and Saint-Germain-des-Prés, the oldest church in Paris. I think I would have to say that everything in me at that time pointed in one direction, to find out what it meant to be a fine artist, to put my life on the line for art, to combine everything I'd learned and everything I felt and then distill that into paintings. It hadn't happened in LA—"the art scene" in LA was crap—but if it were going to happen anywhere, it would happen here. In two years I'd be thirty, and then the whole thing would be ridiculous.

The cab pulled up to the Hôtel du Danube at ten in the morning, and right away I saw I'd made a mistake. The lobby was dark and glossy and touristy, and a clerk my age gave me a chickenshit stare. I asked for their smallest room and I got it—a dark little cubicle toward the back with a single bed, a shorted-out television, an armoire set at an angle on the sloping floor, and wallpaper that went on all the way across the ceiling—brown cabbage roses on a tan background. The one small window looked out on a roof made of corrugated tin.

I felt lousy, but, again, I put that down to jet lag.

After I washed my hands and face I went out for a walk. I knew a run would make me feel better, but I thought I should know where I was running before I suited up and started.

I walked along the rue Jacob to the rue des Saints-Pères and turned up toward the Seine. The sun was out by now. Things looked the way I expected, but not the way I expected. The river was amazing. I could look across it to the Louvre and that was amazing too, more than I could register, more than I could take in. That so many people, so long ago, had been so dedicated to beauty! I thought of LA, weeds sprouting from the sidewalks and retaining walls bulging with dirt from the last earthquake and all the stucco bungalows on the sides of all the hills and how they faded into that beige background of dead ryegrass. I thought of Salvadorean women on Western Avenue with little kids in strollers and more kids strapped to their backs. Everything I remembered seemed monochromatic and sad.

I came back from the river, walking in the direction of the hotel. I thought I should see Saint-Germain-des-Prés, and the famous cafés on the boulevard Saint-Germain. I was getting hungry. Take it a step at a time, I thought. A thousand people, a thousand thousand people have done what you're doing. They got through it. So you can get through it.

Half the people around me were French, but most of the other half were American—hunched together on sidewalks, poring over guidebooks and maps. The French pushed past them. The shops had windows filled with high-class tourist junk—etchings cut out of books and framed, tarnished jewelry you could pick up in LA in thrift shops for ten bucks. And stuff only a moron might want—life-sized stuffed leather pigs.

Saint-Germain-des-Prés was great. Old, old, a mass going on at the far end, groups of Parisians and tourists wandering around in the dark. It calmed me down. I was facing a depressing fact, the fact that I didn't want to go into a place by myself for lunch. I had to remind myself that I was an American, well educated, able-bodied, with enough money to last a while. Picasso had done it (not that he was American). Hemingway could do it. (But thinking of myself at the Ritz Bar in a trench coat might have made me laugh, if I could laugh.)

I came out of the church into the cobblestone yard and looked over to my left, at the café where Sartre and de Beauvoir had eaten lunch every day, if you could believe the guidebooks. I walked off on a diagonal to my right, toward a café that to my knowledge had no reputation at all. I sat down, ordered a *Croque Monsieur,* a *salade des tomates,* and a glass of red wine. Not quite what I expected, because there was a red-faced Irishman stuffing down a pair of fried eggs right next to me, telling a story about the computer company he worked for and how he'd just come in from Hong Kong the night before and how he'd be damned if he'd take the company house out in the banlieues, he'd live in the city or nowhere. On my other side, an American woman in a tight suit explained to someone who looked a lot like her mom that the French were terrific pill poppers, and that she, the daughter, was terribly disappointed that her mother had let herself go, because how could she introduce her to François, when she was looking like that?

Everyone I saw had someone to talk to; everyone had a friend. Everyone had somewhere to go. Everyone had a plan.

I paid my check and walked back to the hotel.

My room faced away from the sun and smelled of mildew and smoke. I pulled off my clothes, got under the covers, and slept.

When I woke up, it was the next morning. I ordered coffee and croissants and the maid brought them up. I sat in bed and ate and began to feel terrible. I got ready for the voices that would be rolling by soon, and sure enough, here they came: my dad, the redneck Texan carpenter who'd taken off when I was fifteen. "You're gonna be a *what?* An artist? Gimme a *break,* Bob!" My mom, sitting alone in her apartment down on Virgil: "That's fine for *now,* when you're still young, but pretty soon life is going to catch up with you. You can't go on living for yourself and expect to get away with it." Living for myself. Man, she was convinced of it.

My old professors: "Hampton, pretty good. No, a B+ is a good grade, especially at UCLA. No, I'm not going to change it. No, I can't tell you what's 'wrong' with the painting! It's just not A work.

I know A work when I see it, and I don't see it here. No, I can't tell you what to do. I can tell you how to get a B, but no one can tell you how to get an A. If I could, we'd all be out on a yacht spending our millions."

Or, "You'd make a fine teacher, Hampton."

Or, "Disney needs animators. You work very rapidly and you're good with detail."

Or, "Did you ever think of special effects? You've got a real craftsman's eye. We're living in the special-effects capital of the world, remember."

But that wasn't what I wanted. I wanted to knock them out. I wanted to knock their socks off. I wanted to change their lives through my art.

Yeah, well.

I got up and took a shower and headed on out to see the Musée d'Orsay.

The day was cold and cloudy and getting inside the museum was a relief: it was warm in there, it was beautiful. The art was something. Manet's *Déjeuner sur l'herbe,* his *Olympia.* How'd he get that light? Renoir's *Dancing at the Moulin de la Galette.* How'd he get that great light?

I went through the museum, feeling worse and worse. The Renoirs—and Renoir wasn't even my favorite painter, for God's sake—made my stomach tie up. I stood for a long time in front of *Danse à la ville* and *Danse à la campagne,* and remembered what one asshole professor had said to me about what I could do to get an A. "You must be born again, Mr. Hampton! You must be born again!"

What if I couldn't be born again? The two pairs of Renoir's dancers—in the city, in the country—showed me a million things in terms of light and technique and even social commentary, but something else in them made me feel like crying like a kid. Some people, somewhere, had been as happy as that.

It didn't matter, because no one in this century painted like that anymore. I tried to remember, back in LA, Tony Berlant using nuts and bolts and metal in all his pieces, doing it for years now. Had Berlant been born again? Born again to what?

I got out of there after a couple of hours and went into a place for lunch, big chunks of veal in a red-orange sauce. I paid too much for it. I went back to the hotel, waited for an hour, went out to a café, and started talking to a good-looking American guy who worked for a French computer firm. Everyone did, he said. Work in computers.

"This is the best café in Paris, absolutely the best. Do you play squash? I make it a point to play three nights a week. Keep in shape. Have to. Going to the École? I have a friend who went there. Best education in France. Absolutely the best. Ever been married? Neither have I. That's the reason I stay over here. They can't get to me here. Not that there aren't plenty of women. *Plenty* of women! How long have you been here? *A day!* I've been here twelve years, off and on. Ex-pat for life, I imagine. Are you free for dinner? Like Greek food? I know an excellent place, right in this neighborhood. Best place in France. Here's Jean-Pierre. Jean-Pierre! Over here! Bob, here, will be going to the École. I told him it's the best . . ."

"Where are you from?" The Frenchman wore a bright red crew-neck sweater and a look like he had a sewer right under his chin.

"California. Los Angeles."

"And you come *here*? That is bizarre. Everyone in France wants to go to Los Angeles. It is our Mecca. We all want to go there."

"More wine, don't you think?" The American guy seemed pretty happy about things. "Greek food tonight?"

The next morning I woke up with a hangover and a feeling of doom. This is it, man! You're here, this is it! Cut the crap, do what you're supposed to.

I crossed the river and headed toward the Louvre. I knew it

was banal or bourgeois, but all I really wanted to see was *The Raft of the Medusa*. Then I'd head out to the École, sign up early if I could, get a newspaper, look for a decent room or maybe even an apartment.

Down in the museum's basement I started to sweat. I checked my jacket and backpack and headed up into wings of art, and more art. Too much of it! Renaissance stuff and pre-Renaissance stuff, and Saint Stephens and Saint Sebastians, and miles of virgins and angels. I recognized everything I'd ever studied and saw a thousand things I'd never seen before. I thought of all the men who'd had something like the same dream I had, *to knock their socks off!* To be born again! Would I ever get hung in a museum? Forget it, I couldn't even get a single show. I didn't even know what to paint.

I heard myself panting for breath. I'd just go see *The Raft* and then head over to the École. I spent another couple of hours looking for the damn thing, if only to know for sure that other people sometimes felt like they were drowning, slipping off, losing it altogether. But *The Raft of the Medusa* was undergoing restoration "due to humidity." It stood behind a tall plywood partition. Just a few desperate arms poking up beyond the plywood. Help! We're drowning over here!

The École des Beaux-Arts had very ornate and wonderful gates. They were closed tight and chained with a padlock. I didn't know why they were closed, but it wasn't going to matter. I pushed my face against the cold metal bars and looked in at the gray, rainy courtyard. Who had I been kidding?

I went back to the hotel, dressed for a run, and headed west along the south side of the Seine, passing churches and buildings and more buildings. Not my home. Not my city. I got to the Tour Eiffel and turned to cross a bridge across the Seine. Was this the Trocadéro?—dozens of black guys my age were selling umbrellas to nobody, shivering in the cold.

I ran back to the Hôtel du Danube, and went thudding through the lobby. I sat for a long time on the edge of the bed, then showered, took a nap, got up again at six, and went to the café where I'd met the American guy.

He'd just come from his psychoanalyst. "I tell him my troubles in French, it's good for both of us. Do you want to have dinner? What about Czech food? Something Italian?"

"Do you mind if I ask . . . how old are you?"

"Forty-two, why?"

We ate Italian, "the best in France." I'd had better on the Santa Monica Promenade. We didn't get out of the restaurant until after midnight, and walked over to the Île de la Cité for ice cream. The city's lights twinkled in the freezing drizzle. We ordered double cones, pistachio and chocolate, and started back another way, and there, on a bridge that separated one part of the island from the other, I checked out maybe a couple of hundred students, most of them American. They sat right out in the rain, huddled up in duffle coats, smoking dope, having a great time. None of them looked up. They were all at least ten years younger than I was. I'd waited way too long. Who did I think I was kidding?

So that was that. I flew back to LA. I'd enroll at the Otis Art Institute in September, brush up on design for a semester or two, get work in advertising, drafting, maybe special effects. Maybe get an MFA, finally, and teach. Figure out something to do for the summer. I'd think of something. On the plane back, I asked myself how I felt. My gone Texan dad gave me the answers: like a sick flea on a pig's butt. Lower than a toad. Wronger than a three-dollar bill.

So I was back again in LA. In late sweltering May there I was again, the way I'd been so many times, at the housing center at UCLA, going over the hundreds of apartments and roommate slots that came up empty at this time of year. I'd had it with the West Side though, and was looking for something else. No more trendoids. I couldn't stand the strain.

I found something pretty quick. A chance at a house, shared with three others, over in the Silver Lake area, halfway up the Micheltorena Hill. A room of my own. Three hundred a month. My old neighborhood from when I was a kid. Picture window in the sunken living room. Ocean view from twenty miles away. Central location.

I drove east from UCLA in my old car, with a feeling of retracing my steps, zooming along Sunset all the way through Beverly

Hills and the Strip and Hollywood, and finally to the western border of the place I'd be calling home again if this house looked OK:
Vermont Avenue, perpendicular to Sunset. Three blocks to the
north, Mom and I had lived for a while in a fifth-floor corner apartment that overlooked The Dresden Room, formerly a pickup joint
for zombies, now too hip for words. There were a couple of book-
stores and a little theater in that same block, but you'd never know
it from my mother's life. She went down to the street to shop for
groceries in the store right below her, and then she went right back
up to sit by the window. Then she moved to Virgil and did more of
the same thing. I tooled through the intersection and tried not to
think about it. No more wide lawns or even straight-up businesses
now, just free-floating weirdness—used-car lots, mini-malls, Vietnamese manicure shops, Korean banks, Mexican restaurants, a
public television station. Sunset Boulevard, still plugging along, all
the way from the beach to downtown LA.

I hit "the Junction," where Santa Monica Boulevard came into
Sunset at a diagonal, and hills sloped up sharply on either side of
me. Sunset was at the bottom of a little valley here, and along the
tops of all these hills old palm trees made a fringe like shredded
lace. It wasn't the banks of the Seine, but if I had a home, this was
it. Amok Books was somewhere around here, and Saint Francis of
Assisi Elementary School over to my left, and in the next block,
Micheltorena Elementary, where I'd gone for a while as a kid, since
Mom and Dad and I had once lived on the south side of Sunset.
We'd lived all over, around here.

The Junction was mostly Mexican now, but it was still my old
neighborhood, seedy, rundown, right in the middle of things, ten
minutes from downtown, and just a look away from the Hollywood
Hills, the Hollywood Sign. You could take wild-card streets like Hyperion over to Los Feliz, which could sneak you around the Zoo
and the new Forest Lawn and out to the San Fernando Valley, or
you could follow Sunset for a few blocks in the other direction,

make a left and end up by Silver Lake itself. People on the City Council liked to live over there.

Central location. Central to what?

I turned left, up Micheltorena, and my hands got damp on the wheel. It was steep! I knew I wasn't going up the whole way, I'd be turning left halfway up on Dahlia, but still, the people who'd laid out these streets in the first place hadn't given a shit. They just eye-balled it and went straight on up. A few blocks over on Maltman they'd shut off a whole city block years ago and let it go back to weeds because cars couldn't make it. I'd played war plenty of afternoons on that wilderness plot when I was a little kid.

This hill had seedy old apartments at the bottom and fancy es-tates at the top, and classy little Neutra houses all along the mid-dle. If you could make it halfway up in this world, you knew you were OK. A little less than halfway up, as I was taking the hill in second gear and trying not to think about it too much, I made a sharp left on Dahlia and there was the house, just a double garage and a front door visible from the street. But a lot of houses were like that on this hill, I remembered that. This one had a thin little stucco lip showing on the street, and probably a big hanging jaw of rooms out back, stuck onto the dirt and hoping for the best.

I rang the bell and after a minute or two a thickset guy about my age opened the door. He wore shorts and a T-shirt, had a big crazy smile and bloodshot eyes. Pretty stoned.

"Come on in. Name's Dave. Show you around."

Very cool in here. Dark and quiet. I peered down a long hall to a patch of bright light, but Dave was moving slowly, giving me the tour. "This would be your room, first one on the left. The middle one is where Austen lives. He's studying for his first qualifyings and his language exam. He's in there now. Hardly ever comes out, ex-cept to organize student strikes. And down in the corner room, Kate. She's a hostess over at Cha Cha Cha. Good Caribbean food. Getting married pretty soon. Here's the living room."

Three steps down, and then a big white room with a couple of chairs and a couch and an old piano. And a good-sized picture window that looked across twenty-five miles of LA to a thin ribbon of ocean.

"Great view."

"Yeah, it's why I took the place. And I like the neighborhood. In transition. That means falling apart. I study over in here."

Three steps back up, Dave had staked out a corner at the dining-room table. "I'm reading all of Adorno right now, are you familiar with his work? No? Want to split a joint?"

An hour or so later, I let Dave get back to his Adorno and began to unpack. Not much to move in. There was already a bed and bureau in what would be my room. All I needed to buy was art supplies so I could work on my portfolio for Otis in September.

Back to being a student again. For what? For what.

Sometime during the hour when Dave and I had been kicking back, Austen slumped out to the kitchen for a sandwich. He'd been soft and sluggy, big and miserable looking, and he hadn't wanted to get stoned. "Got to study," he'd said. Then he'd slumped away again, looking pitiful.

Dave smiled. "Guy doesn't wash much. Stays out of everyone's way, though."

I'd felt pretty good in the little room with Dave, talking about art, about how I didn't know what my real material was supposed to be, but how if all I was really cut out for was to be some sort of graphic arts techno-freak, I'd just as soon pack it in. And I talked a little about Paris. It wasn't as awful as I'd thought it would be, to talk about it. Dave was philosophical.

"Isn't a lot of that Paris myth just a fictional construct? A way we have of placing what we think we want out of our reach? The Paris you want was over by 1925. You're not Picasso. You're—what'd you say your name was?—Bob. Some people might say *this* is the right place to be. For now, anyway."

Driving west a little later on Sunset, still in a pot-haze, I spotted a Ford dealership, and eased on in. If I was back in America I might as well buy American. I needed a van to carry my canvases, I told myself. Plus, I had some sort of idea about being mobile, picking up, getting out, going somewhere, starting over. You could live in a van if you had to. And the Paris money was burning a hole in my pocket.

After a couple of hours in the sun, getting harangued by two guys my age wearing terrible suits, I could at least be glad I wasn't selling Fords for a living. I was embarrassed at how much I liked my Aerostar; but if I were ever the kind of guy to be thrilled, I'd have been thrilled. It was tan, with tan leather seats, and two sets of other seats in the back that folded down to make a bed and clear windows along the sides so people wouldn't think I was a pervert. It was clean and smelled of *new car*!

It was great to make the down payment in traveler's checks, blow off my trade-in, great to watch the sweating salesmen look with big eyes at my bulging money holder. He was the opposite of the clerk at the Hôtel du Danube. I didn't even condescend to haggle about the price. Was this what the great American artist drove, a big tan van? Was this what the great American artist wore, khaki pants and a clean T-shirt and white high-tops? Why not?

I looked in the rearview mirror, and got a grip. Same old face. Brown eyes, curly brown hair, moderately tan skin, medium mouth. I could be a bank robber and rob a million banks, and put a million million bucks in a million numbered Swiss accounts, and no one would ever recognize me, because I was so totally and completely average. I thought of myself in an art-house photo, dressed in a black turtleneck, blowing smoke rings, looking serious, and had to laugh. *"Robert, will you change out of that ridiculous sweater at once!"*

That made me think again of my mom. I'd been staying at a motel since I'd got back, and hadn't told her I was home. I stopped at a coffee shop on Virgil, had a tuna salad sandwich, looked across the street at the apartment where she lived. Dreary, dreary. In all the years the two of us had lived together, she'd never told me I was just like my dad, but she showed it in every sigh and glance. That alone gave me a lot of sympathy for the guy. He'd taken that walk when I was fifteen, literally taken a walk, and never come back. I still kept up with my dad's side of the family. There was a lot of family over on that side, they'd never let me get lost. Over here, on this side, there was no one but my mom.

The apartment house had that old smell. The sad smell of being old. I thought of the Hôtel du Danube. That place was *really* old but it didn't smell as bad as this. I climbed up two flights, went down a dark hall, and knocked. Waited while she decided to open the door.

"Mom. I'm home. It's me. Bob. Surprise!"

"What's wrong? Why are you here?"

"I decided to come home, that's all."

She stood back from the door. "Come on in then."

The same faded furniture I remembered from forever. She hadn't ever bought anything new. She wore slacks and a blouse, and her hair hung limply around her tired face. I glanced across the room and saw what I was looking for—a padded occasional chair with an oval back. It was pulled up to a window. She'd sat in that chair staring down at different streets for years now.

"I've been having this terrible headache. It starts down underneath my left shoulder blade and comes up over my head and ends right here above my eye."

"Ma! Aren't you supposed to be asking me why I came back from Paris?"

"You want to talk about yourself and I want to talk about myself. I don't have to ask you. You'll tell me soon enough."

"Did you take any aspirin for your headache?"

"Aspirin upsets my stomach."

"What about Advil?"

"That's worse."

"What *do* you take?"

"Nothing. My system can't take drugs."

"So. What have you been doing then?"

"There comes a time in your life when you've got to slow down. The things you used to do in your life, you can't do anymore."

I tried a little joke, it was the only thing I could think of. "Ma, you never leave the apartment, so how can you slow down? Like it takes you longer to take a shower?"

"You think because you're young that life won't catch up with you. I'd like to be around when it *does* catch up with you. You think you're too smart to go through what I've been going through, but you're not. I'm all alone, Bob."

"I realize that. I *realize* it! Look, I just stopped by to say I'm back in town, and to give you my phone number."

"You won't be staying here?"

"I found a place over by Micheltorena."

"I would have thought you'd stay here."

"Ma. It's not a good idea."

I looked down at her. Who was to say that life wouldn't catch up with me in the same way that it had caught up with her? She was only eighteen years older than I was, only forty-six, and I thought of her as having been exactly like this for as long as I could remember.

"You wouldn't be so sad if you got out more. I mean it. I'm not kidding."

"I get out."

"No. No, you don't."

She looked away from me. I'd hurt her feelings.

"Look. Who am I to talk? I went to Paris and I couldn't make it, so I came home. So who am I to lecture you?"

"You have your whole life ahead of you."

"Actually, I don't. Actually, I'm getting on in years."

"You're still a young man."

"Not really, Ma. I'm almost thirty! Thirty in two more years."

"Life is an awful thing," she said. "It has so many terrible surprises. I wish there was a way to keep them from happening to you, but there isn't."

"Turn around. Let me rub your neck a little. Maybe it will help your headache. Then I have to be going."

She bent her head and I pressed my fingers into her back. You could have played the guitar on her shoulder blades.

"Not so hard!"

How long it had been, I wondered, since somebody had touched her? Really touched her?

"You ought to try and get out more."

"I'll try."

I breathed the smoggy, heavy air on Virgil like freedom itself. The inside of the van seemed the perfect shelter, everything my mother's place wasn't: clean, impersonal, and new, new, new.

I drove around a while, then found a Kinko's on Sunset. I bought some paper, drew a hammer, a screwdriver, a lightbulb, and lettered:

WHATEVER'S WRONG

I CAN FIX IT

CALL BOB!

I wrote my new phone number over and over at the bottom of the page, then ran off a hundred copies, used the paper cutter to turn the numbers into a fringe, bought a box of thumbtacks, and spent the next two hours inching the van along Sunset, Santa Monica, Vermont, and Wilshire as far down as Hancock Park, putting up my posters on phone poles and car washes and Laundromats.

The heat had broken by the time I'd finished and most of the rush hour had cleared out of the city. I drove back to Micheltorena feeling pretty good. A car and a job. Not bad for one day.

The front door was open and I walked down the long hall to the sound of friendly talk. Through the picture window the sunset across LA looked red and wild. At the far end of the city that strip of the Pacific gleamed like a neon sign.

"Bob? That you?"

"Honey, I'm home," I said.

"Come on and meet Kate. And Austen's even come out for a few minutes."

I walked up three steps to the dining room and there was Dave, eyes still bloodshot, big smile on his face. Austen sat at the table, his mournful head drooping. A smiling girl, overweight but sexy, with nice breasts and sleepy eyes, leaned against a wall.

"I've been trying to get them to tell me what they want for dinner. Not that I'd *make* it! I'm curious, is all. Maybe you can tell me. What do you want for dinner?"

"Come on in," Dave said. "Don't mind Kate. Be part of the family circle. Want part of a joint?"

I checked out the room. "Don't mind if I do," I said. "Man! What a day. Bought a van. Went to see my mom. I'm going to be a handyman this summer. They gave me a cell phone with the van. Customer incentive. I'm drowning in the mainstream."

"Honey," Dave said, "bring Bob a beer. He's had a day."

The crazy thing was, Kate did it. "Just this once," she said. "Don't get any ideas."

3

The handyman job got off to a shaky start. Predictably, some flaky young woman needed me to go to a Hollywood motel, pick up a package, and hand it to her later at the corner of Sunset and Vine. *Sure.* And spend the rest of my fast-fleeting youth in the slammer. Respectable jobs were even worse. Nobody had anything to work with. I spent what was left of my money making shopping runs on Home Depot, picking up a hammer and nails, a couple of screwdrivers, a miter box because my dad always swore by his, and some cans of motor oil in case someone was going to need their oil changed. Trying to be prepared.

My first real job was building a treehouse for a small boy in a deformed tree behind a crummy little house over on Berendo. I thought I did a pretty good job—extending a sturdy four-by-six platform out along the strongest branch, but the kid had expected a regular cottage and threw a screaming fit when he saw what he got. His mom tried not to pay; I insisted on my ten-dollar-an-hour price, and got it. Then I realized in the van driving home that I'd forgotten to charge for the lumber.

One night that first week, I got a call from an out-of-breath woman. "How tall are you?" she asked. "You can't be too tall. What's your inseam?"

I couldn't remember the last time someone had asked me that. Probably never.

"I need you *now*. It's an emergency. Be sure to shower before you come."

"No drug stuff," I said. "I can't stand the stress." But she'd hung up.

I drove to a beautiful art-deco apartment on Wilshire, close to the Ambassador Hotel. A frazzled-looking concierge expected me. "Better make it snappy. Apartment 621."

I heard the argument before I knocked on the door. A drop-dead gorgeous babe in a lamé gown with spaghetti straps looked me over and said, "Fine! Go on in and get dressed. We're late."

"Go ahead and try it, cunt!" Some guy was yelling from the other room. "You haven't got the guts! You'll be the laughingstock!"

"I don't think so. I don't *think* so!" She pushed me into a bedroom where a tuxedo was laid out across the double bed, waiting.

"It's not going to fit . . ."

"It *will* fit. *Because I say so!*"

It did. I looked pretty good, I had to admit it. Even the pumps fit. Patent leather, and they had bows.

She grabbed my arm and marched me to the den. A beaten-down guy peered into his computer, then looked at me with a lot of hate.

"This night's important for me," the babe said. "So Steven picked tonight to lose his brief in the computer. I wonder if he'll manage to find it once we're gone."

"Cunt!"

"Say, listen," I said. I didn't think it was right to speak that way to women. But she ignored both of us. "Bye, now!" she said sweetly, and started out ahead of me, wagging her lamé butt.

As we rode down the elevator I had to tell her, "I only have a van. It's new, though."

I danced the night away with a bunch of Women in Film and their escorts, took a crisp hundred for my pains, and stayed around to watch her pick up an award. I was glad I'd brought my regular clothes along with me in a paper sack. I didn't want to go up to that place again.

I loved the painting and building, but wiring confused me totally. I usually pretended I knew what I was doing, but if it could be moved, I took whatever it was out to an electrician. Generally speaking, I got paid in cash, I met new people, I didn't have to think much. But there was a certain amount of sadness to a lot of this work. Somebody else should have been doing these jobs. I noticed it my fourth day, when some hysterical mother called from King's Road above Sunset to say her daughter had locked herself in the bathroom. Could I come quick, *now*, and take the door off the hinges?

I went right over, thinking a tot might be drowning in the tub, but when I got the door off there was a girl in her teens, her face pushed into a corner by the shower curtain, crying her eyes out. She ignored me completely and asked her mom, "Where is he? Why didn't he come home?"

Her mother said, "He just stepped out of the office. The way he always does. What did you think? Did you think he'd come home for this?"

Ten dollars an hour. In cash. They generally fed me. But I didn't really luck out until the beginning of my second week, when I went to work for a regular family where there seemed to be a lot to do. The Landrys lived down in the flats of Hancock Park on a very well-kept street. The houses were almost-mansions, but not quite. The place had been built in the twenties and needed some pretty serious work. Mr. Landry was a big-time sports agent and hardly ever home. Mrs. Landry seemed nice but disorganized. A lot of the time she was chasing after her son, Tod, who looked to be about three. And there was a great-looking stepdaughter, Millicent, left over from Mr. Landry's previous marriage.

I took a couple of days to tighten up a loose Landry banister, and hang a picture of some Canadian hockey team in Landry's office, and fix all the leaky faucets, and begin a painting job in Millicent's bedroom. Then Mrs. Landry got a bright idea. She hated the white cement around their backyard swimming pool, she said it looked like a bad hotel. This was Landry's house from that same previous marriage and he wouldn't spring for Mexican tile, he said it looked faggoty. Mrs. Landry got the idea, why not paint the cement around the pool—and there was a lot of it—cerulean blue? Not that she had a clue what cerulean blue really was. But then she could buy discount terra-cotta pots over by Olympic and Twentieth, and have Ono fill them with red and pink geraniums, and then maybe I could paint the lawn furniture and the place would start looking pretty good. You could see she had time on her hands.

Two, maybe three weeks' work. Maybe a whole summer. Because in spite of Ono coming over once a week to water and trim, and a chunky little Mexican woman named Conchita who stopped by four hours every morning to clean up, the place was too big, you could see that the whole enterprise was out of hand. The kids were a handful, and the lady of the house was way too far behind.

So I said sure, I'd do the cement. I bought samples of paint from Home Depot, and something made me buy sealant, not just to keep the paint from chipping or flaking, but to see if I could create a great surface. I was thinking I'd do several coats and seal them all. Sure, this surface would never back a fresco, because you had to mix lime and cement with the paint to create a fresco surface and it took fucking forever to do it, and it couldn't ever even be a mural, because murals went on walls, and this was just a huge floor of cement that went for miles around the swimming pool and out to the ivy-covered back fence—way too much cement, because some owner, probably Landry himself, had been too cheap to put in lawn back when he should have, or the tile that would have made the yard look great. All I had to do was paint the cement, but I'd make it a background for whatever might come up. I thought I even might paint on it later. I drove out to Fontana one day and bought marble dust to put in the paint mix. I thought I might make it the greatest blue in the world. What the fuck—I didn't have anything better to do. And I'd have a brush in my hand again.

I thought you could have some dignity painting a white surface blue. Giotto did it; Botticelli did it, plenty of other guys had done it. Even the ceiling at the Sistine Chapel must have had guys like me, not doing the big biblical stuff but painting in the blue, the cosmos. The . . . stuff. Mrs. Landry said she wanted the blue to match the sky in summer. Yesterday she'd said that, then early today she'd looked down into the deep end of the pool, like she was looking for something else, the answer.

"Could you more or less make it match the water in the pool? Enhance it? Make it, I don't know, *more* like the water than the water?"

I liked her a lot, I didn't mind her talking that way. I peered into the pool with her, standing by her but looking sidelong at her forearms as she stood, slanting a little forward, in one of the long brown-and-gold dresses that she seemed to like wearing around the house in the mornings. I looked at her unpolished fingernails with garden dirt under them—in the week I'd been working here, she'd told me about forcing narcissus in the basement and growing flats of jalapeño peppers because the ones in the store weren't hot anymore. I think I already said she had time on her hands. She'd pulled weeds. She'd snipped little pink roses off a monster hedge of them as soon as they looked like they might even think of turning brown.

I had a few samples I was playing around with. I took a brush, four inches wide, stiff bristles, cheap—I was just playing around at this point—and dipped it into the first can, laid a thin margin along the line where some of that white cement met green, stubby grass.

Too pale. Too much like today. June in California. Fog burning off. Not enough color. Going to be hot later, though. I could see taking off my shirt, lying back on white cement, just going *yah!* Scaring Mrs. Landry to death.

Eleven in the morning. Well, I'd been busy. Touched up a place in the bathroom where Tod had thrown his boat at the wall. Weirdo kid. Rousted Angela Landry's stepdaughter, Millicent, out of her fluffy little dream room—which was about as big as a basketball court—white carpet, white bed, white pillows, white this, white that, so that I could give the inside of her dressing-room alcove a second coat of pale lemon yellow. It had been her idea, Millicent's, and I did it in just over an hour, while Millie and Mrs. Landry stayed outside, telling the gardener where to plant flats of perennials.

Millicent wore white satin nightgowns I already knew about, because just this morning I'd seen her yawn and stretch and grin at me and run her fingers through her fine blonde hair as she swung her tan legs so far over the bed that I almost—but not quite—caught a glimpse of *it,* which would have been a treat, but I didn't. "All *right!*" she'd said to her stepmom, on the edge of being really bratty, but not wanting to give up the other glamour thing she was pulling on me. "All right, I'm *coming!* Couldn't you have gotten me up a little earlier?" And then she twitched her slick little boobs right past me, as Mrs. Landry peered into the dressing-room alcove, probably trying to find the answer to a whole other question.

I moved along, crawling backward on all fours, working on the margin between grass and cement. I laid down another blue, and knew right away it was too bright. But unless you tried out the wrong ones, you might not get to the right ones. A white satin nightgown. It made me grin. White silk blouses, white slacks, loose and soft. A stage Millicent was going through. I felt really old, like I'd been through all my own stages.

Too bright. Too raw. Well, I had time to play with this stuff.

I hardly ever saw Mr. Landry. Always on the phone. Television deals. Endorsements.

After barely a week, I knew I didn't like him. I didn't like to look at him. I tried to stay out of his way. Tried not to overlap. I felt very thin and brown when Landry was around.

Sometimes I felt as old as the hills. Man! I felt *older* than the hills. Twelve years older than Millicent, almost twice her age. And what did I have to show for it? What had I ever done? What was I going to do? And on and on. I stood up to get the kinks out of my back, and stretched. A couple more blues to try. I'd lay them out by the other side of the pool. Then I'd knock it off, quit for the day. Head down to the beach. Tomorrow I'd come back and work a full eight hours. In September I'd be back in school. I didn't give a shit because a hundred years from now, who'd *give* a shit?

I put down one four-inch-wide line of deep charcoalish blue that by some magic seemed to have some gold in it. Even though it had to dry and Mrs. Landry had to say yes to it, this might be it. I might not have to do any mixing. It looked to me like a great blue, a perfect blue that might catch some elements of water and air and sky, so that when people came out into this garden they'd see those fat nasturtium borders and white daisies, and new pots of geraniums, everything easy and open. Their eyes would follow the flowers to the deep blue of this—just cement!—and then to the reflecting sky and then down, perfectly, to this small deep pool.

You can see I was spacing.

I stood up and walked over to the edge of the pool. I took a couple of deep breaths and looked the way Mrs. Landry did, into the deep end, kind of absentminded, for the answer.

And I saw Tod curled up at the bottom, with his thumb in his mouth, taking a nap.

I dove in. It couldn't be true, anyway. It had to be a mistake. Tod looked dark, shadowy, a real dark blue. Or it could be a shadow I'd seen, or a joke, or a dog. I came up for breath. Water clogged my lashes, so I could only see light. I went down again. If I weighed more I could have gotten further down. I kicked my legs into the dark, brushed against cloth, came up, and gave it my best shot, dove down again. Maybe it was just cloth, just trash, or somebody had thrown something in. But I grabbed hold of the kid. I held him like a grocery bag, stood at the bottom of the pool, bent my knees, and jumped. We went right up, through the surface of the water into wet sunlight. I couldn't see a thing.

I got to the edge, pushed Tod over onto the cement. I sank back down, I couldn't help it, and took a big breath of water. I'm not much of a swimmer. Then I got out.

"Hey," I said. "Hey!" I called. *"Hey!"*

I couldn't remember any of their names.

I turned the kid over on his stomach, then over on his side. Then I stood up and grabbed him by his heels and shook him good. I pounded on the kid's side like he was a television that wouldn't work unless you gave it a couple of smacks.

Each thing I did brought a little more water out of the kid, until I laid him back down again. He looked dead.

"Somebody help me out here," I said, but my own voice sounded clogged, it was like talking underwater. I watched water draining off the kid onto the cement, staining it black.

"Come on," I said. "Come on."

Another part of my brain clicked in. I remembered going on a date with Tori, some girl from high school, who'd taken CPR. She said first you had to call their name: "Annie, Annie, Annie, Annie!"

I said that, because I couldn't remember the kid's name. I yanked his head back and pushed down his tongue and held his nose and blew into his mouth, but I tried to be careful, because I'd always wondered, watching people do that, couldn't you blow out their lungs? Couldn't you explode them?

I blew again. One, two, three, four, five. I pressed down on Tod's chest. "Tod," I said, and my whole body shuddered. "Tod, Tod, Tod, Tod!" I blew in again. It crossed my mind that it was like kissing a sea urchin, small, cold, soft, wet, wiggly. *"Hey!"* I yelled, "Come out here, somebody! *Millie! Angela!"* But in big houses, it was hard. You never could find anybody. You never knew if they were there or not. A person could die.

"Tod, Tod, *Tod!"* You could say I kissed him again. A junior high school kiss. Pressed his chest. Kissed him again. Dug my fingers into his hair. Pressed his chest. Breathed into him. The kid gave a lurch, and I got a mouthful of crud. I turned the kid on his side, pounded him, spit the crud out into the pool. Green and yellow vomit that floated for a while, then sank to the bottom.

"Come on, *goddamn you!"* I wiped my mouth against the back of my hand, put my mouth over the kid's mouth, remembered to plug that nose, blew harder now. I was pissed. Don't pull this with me, you little shit! I saw the kid's chest move on its own, or thought I saw it.

"Millicent! Mrs. Landry!"

They hung over you all the time when you were trying to work, but when you needed them for anything, they were out getting their nails done, or their hair washed, or trying on track shoes when they didn't even run! Useless, damn useless women. I blew into Tod some more, and pressed on his chest.

It seemed like hours to me. It seemed like the sun had already dried the back of my T-shirt, when finally I heard a high shrill scream like something you might hear at night, a coyote in the hills, and then another, younger scream, like a tea kettle. I knew they were calling 911, and Tod's mom was standing over me. I heard her crying, but I didn't feel like I could look up. I was concentrating now, concentrating like when I used to be painting, really painting, working on a picture that I thought might be good.

So I heard her crying and I could see her somehow off to my side, see her legs through the thin cotton of that brown caftan, and hear the other one screaming away in the front yard, and I heard a big car roaring up the driveway. That would be Landry, I thought, but keep away from this one, Bozo—this one's mine. He did, Landry kept away. He stood there and watched, while Tod's chest every once in a while rose by itself, and an arm or a leg jerked, and his mouth got warmer and warmer and I breathed into him. It was junior high all over again. I thought, it's almost like making out in a movie. I'm getting him warmer now. But no one made out in movies anymore. I'm so old, I thought. Older than goddamn God.

This made tears come out of my eyes. I thought, if I screw this up it will make my life worse than it is now, and I can never come back here. And I can never go anywhere. I kept blowing into the kid, one, two, three, four, five, until I heard the girl, Millicent, out in the front yard screaming like a banshee, and sirens answering back at her. Then the real guys came and pulled me off. I stood up, dizzy and crazy, and looked all around, at the thick hedge that lined one side of the pool and the ivy-covered fence at the back and Landry's plum-colored Cadillac and the big white Spanish house with the red tile roof and the blue sky where the haze had finally burned off and the white wooden Adirondack chairs that didn't seem too far away. I put one foot in front of the other and made for a chair and got there. I sat down, put my head on the warm glass of a patio tabletop.

I knew I cried, but it didn't matter, because there was nobody paying attention. I cried because I knew the kid was alive, but not that alive. He'd been down in that pool way too long. What was it with people, how could they let it happen? I couldn't seem to get over the fact of all the parents who let their kids sink and drown. And right about then I heard Landry in the distance asking, "Who's responsible for this?"

You, butt-fuck! You! I thought, but it made me feel a little better. It meant the kid had to be really alive, up and around, bright as a penny, better in no time, or the dad wouldn't take that tone. I heard the two women saying in some kind of duet, "I thought, *you*!" I even thought, Christ, maybe I was the one who was supposed to take care of him. Then the ambulance got loaded up with the bunch of them, but before that Landry crunched my shoulder with his big jock hand and said, "*Thanks*, son." Millicent knelt down in front of me with her face all tear-stained and said, "You saved my brother's life! I'll never forget you, never!" And beat as I was, I couldn't help noticing those chirpy breasts under her white silk shirt.

Then I felt like I was caught in a vise. A big armful of brown hair covered my nose and mouth and a head pushed on my neck. There was a breast across my chest and another along my back. I thought she might break my ribs.

"Please, *please*!" I said, but Mrs. Landry held on for a minute more. Then she ran off and got into the ambulance, which drove away. I was alone in the yard again. The house stood there as if nothing had happened. The three blues on the cement lay there. I thought again the third one might be the right one.

I walked across the lawn into the kitchen—small, for a house like this—cracked open the refrigerator, and pulled out a beer. I drank about half of it. I noticed my wet shoes were making tracks on the floor so, still a little woozy, I bent over and took them off, put them on the back steps to dry in the sun. I finished my beer, set the bottle on the sink, found another one. It was quiet.

I had to take a piss, and it surprised me. How could anything ordinary ever happen again? How could everything just go *on*? I walked through their formal dining room, past their living room, and found the powder room. She'd said she'd had it redone recently. She couldn't seem to decide what she wanted things to look like. And the house really belonged to Landry.

This room had bad light, the kind that drained you of color in the daylight. I looked in the mirror and my face was like a dead leaf, thin and brown and spindly. My brown hair was close-clipped and looked like Brillo. I didn't look like any de Kooning, Laddie John Dill, Tony Berlant. I wasn't any Ed Ruscha. Kicking back a century, I wasn't any Manet, Monet, Courbet. I wasn't fucking anybody. I looked like my mom, my dad.

And this was what a jerk I was: I was watching myself in the mirror, and it wasn't even my mirror, while a little kid was off maybe dying someplace.

I walked upstairs, found Millicent's room again, went to her bureau and opened the top drawer. Cosmetics, jewelry, tampons, Kleenex. I opened the next, deeper one. Aah! White satin! I slid my arms in.

"Something you looking for?"

Conchita. Concerned and still a little teary. I'd forgotten she'd still be here. But it struck me funny. I couldn't get embarrassed about it.

"Just browsing."

I grinned at her and she grinned back.

But after that there was nothing to do but go. I couldn't stay. I couldn't paint around the pool, for Christ sake. So I had to go. Was this all there was to it? What was it now, two in the afternoon?

I didn't even put my paint and brushes back in the van; it would have seemed like thinking about the wrong things. And I didn't feel like biking or running or going to the beach anymore.

Two of my roommates were home. Kate, and Austen, back from a student strike.

The thing was: in five years, three years, two years, even, Kate would be helping to manage a good restaurant, pulling money in. Maybe she'd become one of those fancy female chefs. She was going to marry her boss at Cha Cha Cha. They'd have kids. It would happen. And Austen would never finish whatever degree he was after, but all those student organizers he hung out with would finally get it that all he wanted to do was protest, and they'd put him in a position where he could really *protest*. And pretty soon he'd be giving speeches and getting on cable television, because there would always be something to protest about. And finally he'd run for mayor. But he'd have to get . . . some good shirts. He'd have to lose some weight.

But me? What was I going to do? Where would I be in five years, three years, two years? I was twenty-eight. Twenty-eight!

I leaned in Kate's door and she put a finger over her lips. "Austen's feeling pretty bummed," she whispered, "He didn't get arrested."

Through the door to his room, I could see Austen lying face down, his legs all over the place, spread out on his unmade bed.

"Tough. Tough luck."

Kate nodded. She was propped up in bed watching the cooking channel on her own TV, the volume turned down low. She wore a bra and some bikini panties under a short kimono. She had a pretty good stomach going there. It was summer, she worked the night shift, so she generally didn't get dressed until late in the afternoon. She lived in the corner room because she paid the most rent. The place was usually littered with spilled powder and opened cologne and thrown-around underwear, but I liked it. I liked her. You couldn't get too lonely with Kate around.

"A kid nearly drowned at work today. In the swimming pool. I saved him. I guess I saved him."

"You're kidding."

"No, I did. I really did."

"That's amazing, Bob. That's great."

"I guess he was down there a long time. I wish I'd seen him sooner."

"You really did it? You got him out?"

"Yeah. I did."

"Did 911 come?"

"Yeah. But he was better by then."

"They say kids can stay under a long time. If it's cold enough."

"Yeah."

I ducked down the hall and closed Austen's door.

"So, Kate? Want to do it?"

"*No!*"

"Why not?"

"Are you crazy?"

"Come on! Special occasion. You can be my hero medal. Don't I get something out of this?"

She gave a last look at the television, where some guy was getting busy with a whisk, and crunched herself up off the bed.

"Your room," she said, "but keep it quiet."

I had the only neat room in the house. The few finished pictures that I still cared about and a dozen new, stretched canvases stored along one wall in wooden racks. There was a painting in progress up on an easel, a bureau as neat as a sergeant's, a twin bed with a white cotton spread, made up and clean.

She fell back on it and looked at me. "Well, come on over then!"

It was like paddling around in a lake, it seemed there was too much of her. Her breasts went all over the place. It wasn't going to be easy. Or, maybe I was wrong. Maybe it would go OK. She grabbed on to my dick and didn't let go, so maybe it would be fine.

She kept sticking her chin up at my face. I realized she'd seen too many movies, she was arching her neck because she wanted to be kissed. (Or felt that was the way it ought to be going.) I was supposed to go all powerful on her, *surmount* her, go over that chin ridge of bone.

But there was so much of her. I really just wanted to put my head down between those big breasts and take a snooze. Her mouth seemed enormous, like the ocean. I tried for the pleasure. Because the bottom half of my body was going along OK, doing what it was supposed to do, so I wouldn't disgrace myself. I opened my eyes to get my bearings, to catch my breath.

Kate's face was broad and sweet. She had pale skin with blue shadows under her eyes. She worked too hard, she didn't get enough sleep. Her hair spread out along the pillow was that curious gray-black-brown. People never say girls have gray hair but they do—that deep charcoal gray. She opened her eyes, smiled at me, and ran one of her hands through my hair. She was so comradely, so friendly, that I almost started bawling. But her other hand slipped my dick in, and I closed my eyes.

Pretend you're drowning. Pretend you're leaving. Pretend you don't live on this earth! And then I did clamp my mouth on hers, trying to get the life back that I'd given out this morning, trying to add onto my life instead of subtracting. Every mouth is every mouth. Suppose this was the way you breathed?

I clicked into another way of thinking, let myself consider Millicent's chirpy little breasts and crackly little bush showing through white satin, Millicent's deep dresser drawer full of white satin stuff, instead of Kate's sturdy white cotton. Millicent's tear-stained face, her fervent *thank you*. I'd heard of contortionists who could go down on their own selves, think how tired your back would get! I felt myself falling where I wanted to go, to the bottom of the pool, getting out, going away, not myself anymore. I remembered getting crunched out of shape, hair in my eyes and mouth, one breast on my back and one on my chest and my vertebrae pushed all out of line by someone so—

"Yah," I said. "Thanks. How was it for you?"

She heaved herself up on one elbow, gently sliding me off her. "Well," she said kindly, "have you ever had a TV dinner?"

"Oh, please," I mumbled. But I didn't feel too bad about it.

"What's the story again? You really saved that little boy? How'd you know what to do? Did you take that course?"

"I don't know if I saved him. They drove off. But I did everything I could think of."

I told her everything, starting from the cans of blue paint.

"You weren't supposed to be watching him, were you?"

"*No!* I thought about that, but no. I don't know who was. I thought I was going to be sick once or twice. I thought he was dead." And I told her parts of it again.

"You were brave," she said. "Not many people could really do that. They'd hop over to the phone and call 911. You were brave."

"Well, it was a *kid!*" But taking everything into consideration I began to feel a little better. Because I'd been feeling like shit.

"Someone should have been watching."

"There's a lot of things in this world that ought to happen," I said, "that don't."

"You did a great thing. You did a swell thing." She locked her arms around me and covered my body with a friendly leg and I began to think we were going to do it again, and I'd give it more attention this time, when Austen knocked on the door and then opened it.

"Isn't there anything to eat in the house? I had some tuna made up but somebody took it."

Austen's face was squashed and fat. His sweatshirt had stains on it, you could see his bellybutton pushing out against the cloth. His sweatpants were filthy, he probably hadn't combed his hair in a week. Kate laughed, and I sat up in bed.

"*Christ,* Austen! No wonder they wouldn't arrest you. You look like a mattress. Think about it. You couldn't get arrested!"

"I just thought somebody might want lunch. You can't spend your whole life fucking around."

Later, while Kate opened more tuna and mayonnaise and rummaged around for bread, I got on the phone. I tried Kaiser and Hollywood Presbyterian and every other hospital I could think of, until I finally tracked down the Landry family and got Millicent to talk to me.

"He's breathing on his own," she told me. "He's got one of those little oxygen things on his nose. So that's good. He opened his eyes once or twice. He hears us, I know. He hears his mom. But they don't know. They don't know. He didn't talk very much anyway. You know, he's only just three. But he's not saying anything now."

4

The next morning I got up early, made my bed, microwaved some oatmeal. How could I go back there? I thought I might understand, maybe for the first time, how my dad could have left. It turned out to be a kind of antimagnetic thing. I'd rather have been any place in the world than where I was supposed to be—down on my hands and knees in the backyard of the Landry place. I put on some paint clothes, walked in my socks past Kate, still curled up in her room, and past Austen's snores to the bathroom. Dave was still asleep downstairs.

"You should have been a great artist," I told the dickhead in the mirror. "That's what you should have been." I brushed my teeth and left. It wasn't even eight when I let myself in through the gate of the house down in Hancock Park and walked out past beds of impatiens and ranunculuses and a carpet of brand X grass to the pool. Too much cement here! How could people be so dumb? Then

I forgot about it and thought about the paint. Once I looked at the colors again, I knew I was right. Even in this early morning light the third blue had depth, you could look down into it.

I began stirring up a batch. I thought I'd give the rough surface lots of coats, play around with more sealant, change it here, change it there, see if I could get a feeling of sea to sky, with clear air captured in it. One of the few good things I could do was play with paint—I had a light hand with it, the way some cooks had with pastry. I could always get air into my work by painting with the grain and then against it. I did that on wood. Cement had no grain, but I could figure out ways to make the color float. As if anybody gave a rat's ass one way or the other.

Around ten, Conchita brought me some iced coffee. I liked the buzz. The June fog burned off early and I took my shirt off. The blue was perfect. I loved it. It drove everything else out of my mind. You could say I worked my mind like a blue scrim. There was stuff behind it but I couldn't see it.

So I was almost surprised when around twelve-fifteen the big Landry Cadillac eased up the driveway and stopped by the three-car garage. I rocked back on my heels and watched as Landry opened the door and Millicent got out of the back seat. On the other side, Mrs. Landry opened the door by herself, pushed the door open with her arm and hip, and got out of the Caddie holding Tod.

Thank God.

I took a couple of steps forward and then thought better of it, as she came around the car and stood with her husband and step-daughter. She held the kid under his rump, cradled his head in her neck. His arms fell loose. Even from here, I could see his eyes were closed. Asleep, from the car.

"I'll sit out here for a while," Mrs. Landry said. "The sun will do him good, won't it, Tod?"

Millicent went inside. Landry kept standing there, looking down at his son.

"Bob." Mrs. Landry said. "Come on over. He's fine, don't you think? A little groggy, but they said we could take him home. He looks good, don't you think? A little sleepy, but they said that's to be expected. They said they did everything they could do. The paramedics said he'd be dead if it weren't for you. So we have a lot to thank you for, don't we, Tod?"

I put down my brush, walked around the pool and put out my hand. "Mr. Landry."

Landry looked at me. "Somebody should have been watching the kid. Was it you?"

"Honey . . ."

He shut up his wife with a look. "I have to know. Was it you?"

But I knew that was wrong. "No. It wasn't me. I worked outside almost the whole time yesterday. Starting by the lawn. You can see where I worked. The first time I saw him was when I looked in the pool." I almost said *I'm not the baby-sitter,* but I didn't. I did say, "Aren't you supposed to have a fence around it?"

"It was Conchita then. She should have been watching. Then maybe this wouldn't have happened." Landry looked down at his wife. "Maybe *you* should have been watching." He headed over to the kitchen.

The kid opened his eyes and saw me. He smiled and reached out his hand.

"Yo! Tod! You had us worried yesterday." I squatted down, took the kid's fist, and had to keep from dropping it. It felt like a salamander. Still wet, clear through. No muscles in the fist. Just damp life.

"Tod? Howzit going, kid?"

Tod smiled and closed his eyes.

His mom held him hard. "They say he's operating at about

eighty percent. They say he's got to have some physical therapy. But that's easy in this city. We've got a lot of it, it's all over. Everybody does physical therapy."

"Did you sleep at all, Mrs. Landry? Don't you think you'd better go inside and try to get some sleep?"

"I'll stay here a while."

And I thought she felt the same way about going inside that house as I'd felt about coming over here this morning.

"The truth is," she said, "we all should have been watching. All of us, all the time."

I heard Conchita shout, and watched as Landry, head down, trotted out to the Caddy, backed it speeding down the driveway, grinding gears, spinning wheels.

"He's . . . having trouble with all this," Mrs. Landry said.

She closed her eyes, her arms clamped around Tod. After a minute or two, I did the only thing I could do. I went back to painting the cement around the pool.

And the crazy thing was, when I looked up once, the kid had gotten loose and crawled over again to the side of the pool. He had his head stuck way over the edge, looking at his reflection, or further, to whatever he thought was down there.

I sprinted over and grabbed the kid. *"Can't you . . ."* What could I say? "Let well enough alone?" I saw that his mom was dead asleep, her lips open, sweat on her forehead. I took the kid inside to look for Conchita. But she was in the maid's room, crying and packing.

"No, not *me*," she sobbed. *"I'm* not going to be the one. That *sinvergüenza,* that hole! I don't stay here. I leave him with his shameful life. I leave him with his pig ways. *Manso,* coward, monster! Let *him* die, instead of the rest. *He* is the one!"

I went upstairs, carrying the kid, looking for Millicent, and heard her talking on the phone. Because of the fancy private school she went to, I knew she must be an old hand at emergency rooms all over LA. Rich kids tried to destroy themselves as a hobby. It was what they used for small talk later on in college. For a minute, I thought like an old fart. I thought that when I was a kid, *if* we'd had a pool, and if *I'd* fallen into it, I would have sunk right to the bottom and died. Because even if there'd been an emergency room around, no one knew where it was, and my mom didn't have a car, and we couldn't *afford* a catastrophe. So I didn't fall into pools, or cross streets without looking. Because I knew better. That's the frame of mind I was in.

"They gave him oxygen, and they gave him some tests, and they said there might be some brain damage, but they don't know. They're going to be sending somebody out to work with him. But he's so little they can't really tell anything yet. Boy! My dad had a spaz attack. But Angela's the *one*. She cried all night."

Millicent was looking at me as she talked, frowning and waggling her manicured fingernails in some kind of hello. "You know who the *real* hero was? Bob. The guy who does a lot of painting around here? Bob is the one who saved my little brother's life. He was a hero, there's no other word for it."

Tod had fallen asleep again in my arms, so I nodded at Millicent, tried out a heroic smile, and backed out of the room. I was familiar with the upstairs. Besides painting that alcove, I'd worked up here hanging pictures, spackling, painting other stuff, firming up that banister. I moved along the polished wood floors to Tod's room, and put the kid down as carefully as I could on his "youth bed," a kind of modified crib covered with stuffed animals.

All over the room were the trophies of being a big boy—posters and pennants from it seemed like every damn professional and college team in the world. That would be Landry's doing. But what would a three-year-old care about the UCLA Bruins and the USC Trojans and the Loyola Lions and the Occidental Tigers? These felt rags were just somebody's stupid hopes pinned up on the wall. Even I could see that these hopes weren't going to be happening.

God, I thought, the kid's only goddamn *three*. Doesn't he get a *train* to play with, or some goddamn Lego blocks? But except for the stuff on his bed, toys were in short supply. Or Conchita had put them away before she hit the road.

Tod slept with his mouth open, looking halfway between a corpse and an angel. Or one of those pre-Raphaelite kids that didn't have any blood in them.

"Man," I said out loud, "this is shit. No kidding." But the whole house ignored me. I could still hear Millicent blabbing on, turning the whole mess into high school chat. And Landry was probably off at his office by now, screwing sports management out of another gazillion bucks, and the lady of the house was chilling by the pool. So the whole conspiracy seemed to be: we will take this little inconvenience and we will absorb it. We won't even see it. What's *your* problem?

I looked down at Tod again, pulled the bedspread out from under him and tucked him in underneath it, so he couldn't get loose without at least a little squirming. Then I walked past Millicent's room, where she was still talking. She waved again as I turned to go downstairs. I went back to the pool and cleaned up my paints, took another look at that mom who was still sleeping, totally zonked, and got out of there. I couldn't stay around anymore. It was just too weird.

But—talk about weird! That afternoon there I was, getting ready for a social event. One of my uncles on my father's side was having a birthday, my uncle Dan. So after a run down Effie Street and out along Hyperion, and a nap and a shower, I pulled out a clean T-shirt and khakis and ironed them while I watched part of an *Oprah* rerun. I found a box of cigars I'd bought at the drugstore a couple of days before, wrapped the thing in newspaper, painted *Happy Birthday Dan* on it, and while I waited for it to dry, went outside and hosed down my van.

Fresh, shaved, washed, I took the van onto the 405 Freeway just ahead of the afternoon rush-hour traffic, heading down past the South Bay Curve through the badlands of Gardena and Carson, where they said the rats at the Carson Mall were big as cats, *bigger* than cats, big as terriers, and down through Wilmington to Seal Beach.

My dad's family spent their summers in a trailer park close to the beach. They loved the lifestyle. There wasn't just one trailer; the family had pretty much taken the place over. Five mobile homes down there had *Hampton* wood-burned on decorative plaques tacked to their outsides. A hundred years ago most of my dad's side of the family had traveled all the way west to Texas by way of Virginia and Tennessee. Then in the thirties they made the big push to California, very proud of the fact that they were one of the oldest failed families in America. My aunt Ada and uncle Jack lived in a shiny silver Airstream from the fifties, perfectly kept up. My two bachelor uncles, Bowlie and Hack, lived in a cut-rate slot off to the back in another Airstream, badly tarnished and dented. Aunt Teresa and her lunk-husband, Otto, and their three kids had moved up to a double wide with plenty of Astroturf carpet inside and a flock of flamingos in gravel outside, beyond parody, beyond anything. I also had a couple of elderly aunts down there, Tess and Vera—still very active in some church or other—and, of course, Uncle Dan and the woman he lived with, Wendy, a nice girl who'd run away from her real husband on her wedding day and worked in the Department of Motor Vehicles.

All these were my dad's family. For a while in the fifties they'd lived in no-down-payment tract homes in Torrance and Maywood, but as Uncle Danny had told me often enough—he'd be sixty-something this birthday—the Hamptons didn't take much to hard work or settling down. One by one they'd slid off and out and back into the trailer culture. They had it pretty good. They spent winters out by Glen Ivy Hot Springs in Riverside, soaking in those springs all day, strolling back down the dirt road they've got out there to their trailer park, drinking margaritas at the bar they had at that place, lying out on air mattresses outside when it wasn't raining, looking up at the stars. Real work wasn't anywhere in it. In June they picked up and headed to Seal Beach, where they'd stay until deep fall. They worked for places like the phone company, or at temp jobs, or handyman stuff. They swam in the morning and got tanked at night, even the churchgoing aunts. My mom had always hated all of it.

But I felt, no matter what, I deserved a family. The Hamptons might not have been the ones I would have picked, but they were the ones I had. And back when I'd decided to go to college, they hadn't bugged me about it. Even when I'd decided to go with being an art major in my junior year, they hadn't yelled at me that I'd never make any money because they'd never made any money, so why should I be any different? They'd tease me every once in a while about turning out to be a nance, but their teasing didn't have any sting in it.

By the time I pulled through the park's rickety gates I could see that the barbecues around the community house were already smoking. Three picnic tables were set up under trees, and there'd be more in an hour or two as beach bums and housewives and people around the park nosed in. I knew the food; I knew the program. Life out of a bad TV commercial, or maybe my dad's family was where those bad commercials had come from. I could already see those half-gallon plastic soft-drink bottles on the tables. I knew hamburgers and hot dogs would be the order of the day, and my aunts' potato salad that was about half hard-boiled egg and choked with relish, and yes, actual dishes of green Jell-O with little marshmallows, and barbecued beans, Dan's specialty, and Wendy's onion dip. Uncle Jack always spent two days making a big pot of chili, cutting up the beef by hand. He'd entered that chili in plenty of cook-offs and never even won an honorable mention, but he loved the stuff and he never changed it. By about ten at night, strangers would drift in stoned to the eyes, and they'd finish it off for him, so it always got eaten up.

I took in the whole road-ness of the scene—Pacific Coast Highway right outside the park, and just beyond that four-lane stretch, the flat pancake of beach. Beyond the sand, the flat dim ocean with gray fog coolly coming in. And right in front of me, the rundown community house with *Happy Birthday Big Dan* on a banner slipping off to one side, and the charcoal drenched in lighter fluid. If I couldn't be where I wanted to be, I could at least sniff the fog and the smoke and let that Jell-O slide around in my mouth and hang out with my dead-ass family.

My aunts and uncles talked about the basketball play-offs, and how the Lakers hadn't been the same since Magic Johnson had played the prima donna and let the championship slip through the team's fingers because of his boring AIDS. "It's because he's so into *It's my last chance,*" Dan said. "He's in, he's out, he's in, he's out. He wants everybody else to forget the AIDS thing, but *he* can't forget the AIDS thing. Like he's the damn poster child. He ought to grow up."

Aunt Tess and Aunt Vera pursed their lips. I didn't think I could stand to hear some churchly rant against homosexuals, but it turned out to be my aunt Teresa who nursed a grudge, for another whole reason. "What I want to know is, what happened to all the women—men too, maybe—that the man slept with? How many people did he infect? Did he pay them off or what?" Teresa, God, I could remember, used to be beautiful. Now her face looked like a gravel bed, splotchy and sad. I wondered what my dad looked like now, if he was still around.

I looked over at the guys at the table: Otto, Teresa's lunk-husband, stared across PCH at the ocean; Dan looked at his unopened presents in a sort of noncommittal way; but here were Uncle Bowlie and Uncle Hack, lighting kitchen matches one after another, giving me big silly grins. What was *that* about?

It didn't feel right, so I slid off the picnic bench and went to look for somebody to play a little volleyball with before dinner got started.

It wasn't until much later, after a long game, and a bunch of hot dogs and some of Jack's bad chili and a couple of joints kept half-heartedly out of sight of the aunts—not until we polished off the cake with sixty-three candles on it, and took care of the melting ice cream on paper plates; not until someone turned on the lights outside the community house and everything started gleaming in a foggy yellowish haze, and a bunch of other people had dropped by to wish Dan a happy birthday and stayed to eat and drink, and that bad chili was finally getting eaten up, and some music or other was blaring away, that I saw Bowlie and Hack looking sideways at me again, smiling flirtatiously.

I thought, I've got to stop smoking this stuff because it makes me paranoid as hell. I smiled nervously at my bachelor uncles and thought about getting up and getting out of there, but I was too stoned. Instead, I focused my eyes on the table where party wreckage made some interesting designs, the paper circles and crumpled napkins and the arms and hands of all these Hampton guys as they held, or didn't hold, their beers . . .

Uncle Bowlie passed me a note. *Want to burn up a building tonight? Fifty bucks for you?*

So it turned out that it wasn't Tess or Vera or Teresa or Wendy who had the righteous tantrum, but me, Bob, standing out by my uncles' ratty old trailer trying to make sense of it all but yelling, yelling like a fool, saying, "Why didn't you *tell* me?" and Bowlie suggesting, reasonably enough, "Well, kid, we *are* telling you. That's what we're doing."

I was pretty stoned and way out of control. "How long has this been going *on*?"

Bowlie said, "Long as I can remember. Live in a house, burn it down, collect the insurance. No problem. We had to branch out though. No more houses." He gave me a game little smile.

"There's no harm to it," Hack said. "Nobody gets hurt."

"Does everybody *know*?"

"Well," Bowlie said, "sure. Everybody's got to make a living. Don't go all prissy-ass on us."

I turned and trotted back through the park, past the party that was still going on, and got into my van and gunned the motor. I drove back up the 405 and turned right at the 10 to head back home, but I couldn't do it. Instead, I turned off on Wilshire and saw that I was going to be driving back into Hancock Park. And there I was on Sycamore, cursing myself for a fool, knowing that a strange guy in a van after the sun went down was bound to be picked up here by the cops. Then I'd be a criminal like the rest of my family.

It wasn't even midnight yet. Quite a few lights in the neighborhood were still on. I parked on the street across from the Landry house. The moonlight was bright. I looked at the bland white façade, the smooth lawn, the brick path up to the front door, the arbor that supported the wisteria Mrs. Landry liked and that I'd already tried to anchor to the second story. I stood against my van and waited, watching for movements on the second floor. The light was on in Tod's room, and in Millicent's. There went Mrs. Landry, carrying the kid. I went on waiting, maybe a half hour, maybe more. Lights along the street began to go out. People watching *Nightline* or *Charlie Rose* decided to call it a day. Tod's light went out. And a hall light, dim and further on in the house somewhere, out. Finally, Millicent's. The master bedroom faced the pool, but they had to be asleep too. I knew their bedroom, quiet and big.

My neck was getting stiff, and I was starting to shiver. But I couldn't seem to get back into the car. I'm going to, I said to myself. I'm *going* to.

Then, like a pretty picture in a frame, maybe a Fragonard, there was Millicent, her blonde hair curling all around her face and catching the moonlight, her skin showing up dark against that white satin nightgown she was wearing. She leaned her elbows against the sill and checked out the moon and the neighborhood.

Of course she spotted me.

She waved a big wave and gestured at me to come on over. I walked across the lawn, feeling stupid, and she whispered down to me, looking positively thrilled, "Come on up!"

"How?"

"The arbor!"

I knew how shaky the damn thing was, but I certainly wasn't going to be able to walk away now. I shinnied up the strongest pole and felt the whole structure creak. I thought of the Hancock Park security cops, thought of Landry, the irate householder, waving a gun. Then I pulled my body to the top of the arbor and more or less danced across it over to the window where she was waiting to pull me in. I was covered with twigs and leaves and blossoms, and I shook myself like a wet dog as I stepped inside. Not very romantic.

"I'm an orphan," I whispered. "I don't have a family anymore."

Even then I wasn't sure what was going to be up. Was she going to tell me about her troubles at school? Or dish about her stepmom? Or get sad about her little brother? Or just listen to my own sad story? Because I was getting ready to tell it.

But it didn't look like it was going to be any of that. She pointed to the door to the hallway, and twitched her fingers to show it was locked. She tiptoed over to her bed—white and puffy and covered with pillows and flounces—turned the sheet down on both sides, then jumped on in, her hands clasped around her knees. I thought of Mr. Landry, mega-agent, and my own hands got damp.

"Hey!" I whispered, "Get out of that *bed*! I'm gonna get my ass whipped by your dad!" Of course, *I* was the one who'd danced across the trellis in the goddamned middle of the night, and come in the window, and hung out like a vagrant in front of the house, just waiting for the security cops of Hancock Park to cruise by and pick me up. But I was trying to stay on the high road.

Millicent patted the sheet beside her and gave me a terrific grin. The moonlight brushed over her like an egg-yolk glaze; the light caught her teeth, she was her own light show. Amazing! Amazing that I should be here with this beautiful girl.

"Come on over!"

"This is a bad idea," I whispered, kicking off my shoes and sliding onto the fresh-smelling sheets. "This is a *terrible* idea. I've got to be getting out of here right away." But just thinking of that arbor made my heart sink. I knew I'd plunge through going back down. I could see it in my mind's eye—the cops zooming up, Landry storming out, poor Bob Hampton sitting in the middle of the lawn covered with flowers and splintered wood. They'd put me in jail. They'd shoot me full of holes.

Meanwhile, my right hand had begun to run, all by itself, along the silvery curves of her slick little body. She was muscular and twangy, of course she *would* be, she was Landry's daughter. Even her breasts had a springy give to them.

"How old are you anyway?"

"Eighteen?"

"I don't think so!"

"I'm going to be a senior next year. Then I'm going to USC." She'd wiggled over next to me, she was practically under me now.

"Don't you, don't you, have a boyfriend?" I said this into her neck, my nose cushioned by banks of her blonde hair, my lower lip brushing her fragile collarbone.

"Not really. Don't talk."

"Wait, though. Wait a minute." I reached in my back pocket, pulled out my wallet, found a condom, a couple of them. "I hope," I whispered, feeling like somebody's grandfather, "that you always remember to ask for these. It's very important."

My legs were pulling themselves out of my khakis and briefs, my arms getting rid of my T-shirt, my body sliding down against the sheets. She turned on her side and grinned at me.

"Isn't this *cool*?" she said, and I said, "Sshh."

It was like being caught in a brisk wind, like being out on a long sail in a choppy sea. I'd reach for her, she'd reach for me, I'd pin down her arm, she'd pin down mine, I'd reach for her breast, she'd turn onto her stomach. I began to think she really hadn't done this all that much. She wound up on her back, finally, and I jumped on top of her and held her shoulders in one place with my upper arms. Then it was done and I came to myself in a sweat, sick about how much noise we might have made.

It didn't seem to bother her at all. She snuggled down in her pillows, ready to jabber.

"You know, he looks like he's going to be OK. He's kind of strange, but he was always kind of strange. Like he never did get out in the sun enough? He has this transparent look? Daddy always wanted a son, that's all he could ever talk to me about, that I was fine for a daughter, but a man needed a son—write a poem, plant a tree, have a son, *you* know. That's some Spanish proverb, boy did I hear *that* when I was growing up! So now he's got this new wife, she's not so bad. To tell the truth, she's pretty nice, and she puts up with him pretty well, but now he's got this new, actual son, and from the minute he saw Tod, you could see my dad was disappointed in the whole thing. It was a son, but not the son he wanted.

You could just know, looking at Tod, he was *never* going to play catch with anyone, and now he *sure* won't, but he never would have anyway. My dad, he's a nice dad, and I love him, but he's *limited*, he's got these serious limitations, so I try to just love him the way he is, and I appreciate that he wants me living with him because my mother gives me a pain actually, she's the type who has fat taken from her butt and gets it pushed into the backs of her hands so she'll look like a teenager? But she's not a teenager, *I'm* the teenager, and she's got this underwear that she orders out of really good catalogues, because even *she* knows she's too old to try it on in stores. She *won't* grow up, she just can't, and my dad, even though he's kind of a geezer, at least he's a pretty OK man, so I'm glad I'm living here, and Angela's OK, she's quite nice, and I love Tod, he's a little sweetie, he's just the sweetest thing . . ."

I stretched out flat on my back and looked at the ceiling while she went on. I knew I ought to be thinking about noise and I did, for a minute, but then I thought, she's on the phone all the time anyway. If they hear anything they'll just think she's on the phone, because isn't she always on the phone?

I knew I ought to be thinking about getting out, but I was just so comfortable.

"Seeing Tod like that made me wonder about his soul. You know, when he was almost drowned, and you were working on him? And they say the soul goes out of its body? Where would a little soul like that go, if he's only three? Actually, he just turned three. Don't you think he'd be watching you and thinking he'd have to come back because you were working so hard? And he decided to come back because it would hurt people too much if he didn't come back?"

I felt myself drifting off. I'd have to leave soon but my whole body felt like it was melting right down into the sheets. I sniffed a little. Smelled sex and bubble bath and clean sheets and detergent.

"But what does that say about little kids in Peru who've got that nutrition disease where their hair turns red and they just die like flies? They have souls too, they must have, they've got to. But nobody worries about where *their* souls go! Do you think that's a *Christian* thing, that you've got to have an identity before you can even have a soul?"

She shook me awake. "Did you know they're sending Mormon missionaries down to South America, and they think that those original tribes they've got *rowed* across the Atlantic from Israel a long time ago?"

She shook me awake again. "Don't you think you'd better get out of here? You're going to get into trouble!"

In the morning sun she looked perfectly bright and fresh. Her nightgown didn't even have a wrinkle.

"Oh, God." I pulled on my clothes and looked out the front window. "Oh, *God.*"

"Just go on down the hall. They're all still asleep. But you'd better get *on* it."

I crossed to the door, opened it up, closed it, and began walking down the hall. Of course Mrs. Landry saw me as she came out of Tod's room. She must have been in there most of the night.

"You're here early. I'm glad. I've got something else for you to fix." She beckoned me into Tod's room where the poor little kid lay tucked into his youth bed, surrounded by those stuffed animals of every size and shape.

"His lamp broke last night. It isn't the bulb, it's something else. The wiring. He loves this lamp."

The base of the lamp was Grumpy the Dwarf. I took the lamp and wrapped the wire around it.

"You probably want to fix it downstairs. So Tod can sleep."

"Sure."

I worked an hour on the damn lamp, then I said I had to go out on an errand. I took the lamp to a repairman who fixed it in five minutes. I stopped off at McDonald's for some coffee and an Egg McMuffin, then headed on back to the Landry house, where I dropped off the lamp and laid down another coat of blue along one side of the pool.

Around noon, I drove home to get some more sleep, but the messages were piling up. It seemed like everyone in LA needed something fixed.

The Walker family lived above Los Feliz, in the hills, in another of those massive, white stucco Spanish jobs. I pulled up in front and checked the address, but I recognized the place before I found the number. The lawn needed mowing. Windows along the front of the house hung open any old way. The gate to the back slumped. I sat in the van a minute or two, feeling stretched all over from my night with Millicent. Then I heard a piercing scream—from the Walker house, of course. I took a deep breath, opened my door, and got out of the van.

"I'm Bob Hampton. Handyman?" I smiled at the woman who began tearing at my T-shirt and gulping like a fish before she choked out, "In there, in *there*!" Then she gave it up and began to scream. Again.

The living room was huge and ugly, full of kelly green furniture against ivory wall-to-wall carpet. But she was waving me into the dining room, where a couple of middle-sized kids pushed at each other. A big refectory table had old food and dishes all over it and up against a wall a very big reticulated python writhed around in a glass cage.

"I *told* you," Mrs. Walker raved, and lunged at the boy, "I *told* you, Hugh, never, never . . ." She began to scream again. "Aaaaaaaah!"

Hugh caught his mother's drift, dodged her sweeping hand, and his sister took it—right on the chin.

"Samaaaantha! Get out of the waaay!"

But the little girl, chubby and about ten, with a lot of macramé on her dress, decided to stand her ground and scream back at her mother.

"What's up?" I said. "What's going on? Is there something I can do?" I noticed that while the two females were howling, Hugh had withdrawn a little, folding his arms, trying not to snicker. "Can I do something?"

"The rabbit got loose," Hugh said. "The snake needs his lunch. Uncle Sam is hungry."

"I *told* you, Hugh! I *told* you! Never, never try to *feed* him!"

Hugh smirked and Samantha looked confused. Mrs. Walker stopped to take a breath and then let loose again. Samantha and her brother listened to their mother's screaming along with some appreciation. It really was kind of an art form.

"Ma'am? Ma'am? Could you"—I had to raise my voice—"could you tell me where the rabbit is? Do you want me to try to find the rabbit?"

Mrs. Walker whacked Hugh, got him straight this time. The kid staggered and felt the side of his face where his mom had clipped him. He looked over at me with a lot of outrage, and then he began to roar.

"You *criminal*!" He yelled at his mom. "This is *child* abuse! I'm calling the cops! Right *now*!"

"Just *try* it! Eeeeeeee!"

In the middle of all the noise, Samantha looked at me and gave me a shit-eating grin. Then she pointed to the corner of the room where a mangy rabbit sat, looking pretty sick.

"It jumped out of the sack. I told Hugh he shouldn't be doing it, but he did it anyway, and the rabbit got out."

"God, it's just a poor little rabbit. A live one!"

"They have to be alive or the snake won't eat them. Snakes don't like dead things."

Mrs. Walker and her son went on screaming. Hugh, by this time, had got into a pretty loud groove.

"So what is it I'm supposed to do? Give the rabbit to the snake?"

"Yes. *She's* afraid the snake will get out. It's happened a couple of times before."

Mrs. Walker grabbed Hugh by the arm and the two slammed together up against the table. "Insolent, impudent, I'll show you! I'll *show* you!" Hugh didn't seem to be hurt, but he yelled over to me. "Look what she's doing! Be my witness! Call the cops! Call the *cops*!"

I walked over to the rabbit and picked him up behind the ears. "I'm sorry, buddy," I said, and carried him over to the cage. I slid open the top with my left hand and tried to drop the rabbit off my right, but the rabbit loved life more than I gave him credit for. He turned just enough to hold onto my forearm with his back paws. I tried to shake him off, but he wouldn't budge.

Then the snake bit me on the wrist. It hurt like hell.

"*Shit!*"

Hugh and Mrs. Walker stopped screaming and started to laugh. The snake went after the rabbit, who came running right up my arm. The snake went after it, up my arm, and across my chest.

Mrs. Walker began to scream again. "He's getting out. I *toooold* you! He's getting *ooout*!"

I grabbed the rabbit with my right hand just as it made a last-ditch attempt to escape down my left arm, and threw it into the cage. The snake had to stop and think about this. He was still wound pretty tight at the tail around my right arm. He reared back from my chest and gave me a long look. Then he decided, fuck it, it was just a hobby, went slipping back down into the cage, and gave the rabbit an evil eye. The rabbit settled down to wait for the worst. I slid the glass back and clicked the cage shut. I was dripping blood all over the place.

"Be sure he doesn't get out," Mrs. Walker said. "We want to be sure he doesn't get out. He's done it before and we had to call the Fire Department."

A half hour later, after they'd bandaged my hand and given me a couple of cold beers, I stood in the laundry room while Mrs. Walker talked.

"I got a little behind. Michael says there's no excuse, that I don't work outside the home, so it ought to be easy. But I'd like to see him try it! Blanca quit, Rosario quit, and Candelario quit. There's only me. There's only *me*!" She began tuning up to cry again. "It's those damn kids! They don't give me any help. They don't give me any respect! I can't do it. I *won't* do it! They can do anything they want to me! But they can't make me *do* it!"

The room we were standing in had about two feet of dirty clothes on the floor, wall to wall. I bent down, picked up an armload, opened up the washer, jammed the clothes in. Not exactly handyman work, but what the hell. "Detergent?" I asked. "Do you have some around?"

"I don't *know*!"

I found some on a shelf, and started the washer. "Ten dollars an hour," I said. "And I got here at two."

I went into the kitchen, which was a shambles.

"Dishwasher?"

I saw it as I was talking and began loading up. There was so much junk and crap and dirty dishes and old food on the sink and on the center counter island that I didn't have to move to load. I just reached and reached and reached, filled the machine, found the other detergent, started it up.

I began at one end of the kitchen, clearing the way, putting dead food down the garbage disposal. I ran hot water in a bowl, poured in some Clorox, found a sponge, and began wiping my way inch by inch down the long counters. Hugh and Samantha came in and watched.

"Make yourselves useful, will you, guys? Bring in the dishes from the dining room. Stay away from that snake, now!"

They looked at me like they'd been debrained. Then they turned around to get some dishes.

"Put them on one of the counters. Any counter. That's cool." I got maybe eight more inches closer to the sink, driving the mess in front of me. "So, Mrs. Walker? Things got a little out of hand here?"

She nodded her head, but she wasn't going to say anything more.

"Can you put that load of wash we just did into the dryer?"

Her eyes filled with tears. She shook her head. "No. I won't."

"No problem. Forget it. I'll do it."

I put the clothes in the dryer, and tossed another load of dirty stuff in the wash.

"What's your first name, Mrs. Walker?"

"Jamey."

"So, *Jamey*, what's the problem?" I didn't look at her, I kept my attention down on the sink. I asked her again, "What's the problem? How long has it been like this?"

"Ever since, ever since . . . I can't be the only one," she said.

"Can't be the only one *what*?"

"There isn't any . . ."

"Yeah?"

"There isn't a . . ."

I came upon a dish of what looked like Stouffer's spinach soufflé, something my mother used to fix for herself, but it was actually a dish of mold. I put it down the disposal. I couldn't hear her over the grinding noise.

"What?"

"Reason to live."

She was maybe forty, her wild eyes were a very bright blue. Her skin looked tight and tan; she'd probably had a lift. I don't think I'd ever seen a sadder face in my life.

"Jamey. Don't feel bad." I put my arm around her and patted her shoulder. Hugh and Samantha stared at us, goggle-eyed.

"You kids. Keep those dishes coming. Jamey? Are you divorced or something?"

"Business trip. Michael's coming back tomorrow. That's why I called you. But that's . . ." She took a long, shaky breath. "That's not—it. I've got . . . there's no reason for me to . . ."

"Don't think about it now. Why don't you look in the fridge and hand me any bad food you see, OK? You kids! Go upstairs and see if there're any more dirty dishes up there. Just do it. When's Mr. Walker coming back?"

"I *said*. Tomorrow. Around noon, I think."

I worked five hours steady. I set Samantha to folding laundry, and sent Hugh—who gave me a certain amount of lip—out to mow the front lawn. At about five, I could look around the kitchen and decide that it was clean enough. My hands were Clorox-soaked and wrinkled. I felt as tired and crabby as any housewife. Mrs. Walker hadn't been good for much. She sat at a table and watched me the whole time, sniffling a little, and rubbing at her eyes.

"If Rosario and Candelario hadn't quit, this wouldn't have happened," she told me at one point.

"Yeah, but if you're going to go around yelling like that . . ."

"You don't know a thing about it!"

"I do, though. I do."

By eight that night, the place looked OK. I took my money in cash.

"Tomorrow morning you want to go out and get your hair done or something, then you'll be up to speed," I told Jamey. "And kids, make your beds before you leave for school. That way it'll look good for your dad."

"Ah, who cares," Hugh said, but Samantha said, "Bob? Are you ever coming back?"

"Ask your mom," I said. Mrs. Walker looked skeptical. It seemed as if she might be homesick for the dirty clothes and old food.

They walked me to the van, but on the way, brushing by a wall of ivy, Hugh heard a scuffling noise. "Look! Mom! There's a possum in the ivy! Quick! Let's see if we can get him out!"

"Bob!" Mrs. Walker screamed, and dug her fingers into her hair, "Bob! *Looook!* There's a possum in the ivy!"

But I wouldn't look. There was no way they could make me look. I hopped in the van, made a daring U-turn, and skidded down Vermont, past Los Feliz, and back again into the land of the marginally sane.

CHAPTER

6

Within the week, Dave and Austen and I were looking for another roommate. Kate finally moved in with the owner of the restaurant where she hostessed. Her corner room was left clean and empty, a lot better than the room I had. I considered making a run for it, but my own room was already filling up with house paints and art paints, and the closet worked as a storeroom; it wasn't worth the trouble.

Austen's middle room smelled like a dog had died in it. And any-time of the day or night when I walked by Austen's door, I could hear him groan, groan in the most terrible way.

"What the *hell* is he doing in there?" I asked Dave one after-noon, but Dave had his reference books around him and a chess game going with himself and a Walkman at the ready in case he needed some music, and a stack of ham sandwiches and a pitcher of lemonade and a bag of chips, and a hand of solitaire laid out. He only smiled. He got a kick out of Austen.

"He's using the summer to study for his German exam but he can't stand to give up his groundbreaking work on Australian aboriginal syntax, and he can't keep two foreign languages in his head at once. That's what he told me, anyway. Plus, he keeps organizing Hispanic students on campus and they don't respect him because he's not Hispanic. So he groans."

Dave gave me another big smile. "That's why I keep my amateur status. Take only extension classes, or ones down at City College. A life of learning without the agony. As if there were any jobs, anyway! For a linguist? A philosopher? I don't think so, laddie."

I hesitated. It wasn't for me to ask. It wasn't any of my business. But I asked him anyway.

"You make a living now, don't you?"

"Layout. Take-out layout."

"I'm sorry?"

"Those ads you see in the paper for ten million television sets at Adray's, or fifty million CD players at Circuit City? I do those ads. The regular advertising guys hate to do them. I've got a network of places that know my name. I could work forty hours a *day* if I wanted to."

"But . . ."

"But what?"

"Do you . . ."

"Do I hope to make something of myself someday, young man?"

"I guess."

"Yeah, I do."

"I guess I meant—what do you want to do later?"

Dave reached over to a pitcher and poured himself some lemonade. "If something doesn't happen by the time I'm thirty, I guess I'll have to do something. But I think I have that much time to figure things out."

"Things?"

"I want to figure . . . what's the right stuff to be doing. Which is why I majored in philosophy. But it's not the theory I care about. When I read *La Nausée,* I get distracted. Like, why does Sartre hate the bourgeoisie so much? What's wrong with Sunday lunch in a restaurant after church? When I was in Paris, I noticed he got himself a big bourgeois tombstone right next to Simone de Beauvoir, you know what I'm saying? He didn't have any qualms about that."

"When I was in Paris . . ."

"Not the place for me. But, hey, what *is* the place? Isn't that one of the things a man should figure out first? And then, who is the woman? The right one, I mean. And what's the right work? And will all that make you happy? Or should we even want to be happy? And how much do we serve the community, or should we even bother? If we can manage to be totally self-sufficient, maybe that's a service in itself. Like, I have everything I need in this room except for a place to sleep, and that's right downstairs."

"No girl, though."

"If I wait long enough, the right girl will come. Or I'll have to go out and find her. She could be right around the corner."

"No friends?"

"I sat here and thought about a friend. And you came in. And there's always Austen."

I had to laugh. "Do you talk to him like this? No wonder he groans!"

"No. I don't talk to him like this. The guy's barely holding on."

"What are you going to do about the room?"

"I had the guys over at the housing office put up a notice for a female. We need one to civilize the atmosphere. What I'm doing is conducting an exercise in human behavior here. What's the best way to live? I've already figured—you need a house with a female in it."

After what I'd already seen this summer, I had to wonder about that. LA had plenty of houses with women in them. It was the men who seemed like they'd all stepped out for a smoke. And could anybody anywhere pass Mrs. Walker off as a civilizing influence? I sat down at the table, looked around, got up, went to the kitchen, came back with a glass. "Can I have some of that lemonade?"

"Sure."

"I used to think that life without art was useless. That life without art was the way my family lived."

"Yeah?"

There was no point in telling him how bad I was feeling. "Otis wants a portfolio. A minimum of twelve pieces, including four to six drawings from life—a self-portrait and some still-life drawings. And pieces that show my 'color sensibility.' I guess I have the whole summer to think about it. But I . . ."

"You know what I've been thinking? Plato envisioned a city, but he didn't care about building it. I've thought it might be interesting—fun—to be a city planner, but any city planner you meet is a bureaucrat in a gabardine suit. All he can think of is how to build a promenade so pedestrians can buy coffee. I'd like to hit that place in the middle where you've got the material *and* the idea, and they come down together. Like finishing up your bacon and your pancakes at the same time."

"Yeah, but what if the people you're working for don't like bacon or pancakes?"

There didn't seem to be much more to say. But it was OK just sitting with Dave, looking out the window. Four-thirty in the afternoon. Watching the eucalyptus leaves in the sun. Maybe I'd work a little on a self-portrait later. The last thing on earth I felt like drawing or painting was myself.

Then the house shook. I think we both figured it was an earthquake. Some other kind of explosion? For some reason I noticed a line of bright-colored crockery on the sideboard, pottery mugs that had jumped a good quarter of an inch. Bright yellow. Deep pure green. Turquoise. And the greatest red, looking like it came straight from the clay it was made from.

We heard footsteps in the kitchen. "Hello? *Hello!*"

"Out here," Dave called.

"The least you could have done is answered when I said hello."

"Didn't we answer?"

"Not until I forced the issue."

She stood about five-four and weighed maybe a hundred and ten. Her brown hair was pulled back across her great big head with plastic barrettes, and her forehead was shiny with sweat. Her eyes were small and a slab of bright red lipstick waggled around on the bottom half of her face as she talked. She was wearing a brown suit that could break your heart if you thought about it, a definitive shit brown that carried a green sheen like ham that's spent a month in the sun. Brown lace-up oxfords. Where did she even find shoes like that?

"Are you looking at my breasts?"

"No!" I said.

"I am *not* a sexual being to you!"

Dave seemed to remember his position as rent-taker and philosopher in this house and tried to get the upper hand. He did it the wrong way, though.

"What the fuck are you talking about?"

"Don't you use profanity with me! I'll be writing to the housing office as soon as I get settled in."

She looked like a certifiable nutcase. She couldn't stand still. Her arms jerked around all over the place, her eyes rolled in her head, and her big red mouth gaped. She had good teeth though. The suit was the problem. She might have looked OK without the suit.

"Just go on doing what you're doing! You're *asking* for it!"

"The housing office sent you?" I was trying to keep up the conversation.

"What do *you* think, moron!"

"But . . ."

"Is someone going to help me with my cartons? Show me my quarters?"

Dave tried to assert himself again. I could have told him it was a losing proposition. "Don't you want to take a look at the room first?"

"A *room? One room?*" She started waving a three-by-five card. "I was told this was a three-bedroom home with another room in the basement and a double garage and a view of Catalina if the weather is good, a kitchen, dining room, and sunken living area. I demand full access to every room in the house, and fair rotation on the parking spaces!"

"I don't think you want to stay here." Poor Dave, again.

"If you *try* to tell me that this room is already taken—"

"OK. *OK!* I'll show it to you. Bob, you want to come with us?"

"My parents know where I am, you know. So does the housing office. Don't think the two of you can try anything."

But Dave was already up and out, cutting through the living room and up into the hall to Kate's old corner room. I followed along after both of them.

"This is it."

It really was a great room, with sunlight and eucalyptus and scotch broom and morning glory just outside the windows. A double bed, bureau, good mirror. Kate had left it looking good.

"There's a bullet hole in the wall!"

I wished I could draw with the speed of light, and capture the look on Dave's face.

"Right here!" She scraped at the stucco with a stubby fingernail. There was a bullet hole all right.

"I demand a different room."

"This is the best one in the house. Bob should have taken it, but he didn't want to move his paints."

She turned around to me, pushing out a bony hip in my direction, and spread her big lipstick mouth over that great set of choppers. "Oh, do you paint? How inspiring!" Her poor suit was so stiff it didn't bend along with her.

"Would you like to see my room? You're welcome to it."

We walked down the hall, the three of us. It was like escorting a short circuit.

"This is a *dungeon*," she said, and gave me a sour look. Then she said she had to see Austen's room. After a low warning knock, Dave opened it.

"Go away," Austen moaned. "Leave me alone."

After the door was closed, the girl sniffed. "That's *disgusting!*"

Dave made his way back to all his junk in the dining room. "So, do you want the room or not?"

"What about the downstairs?"

"The downstairs is mine. You can write a letter of protest to the president of the United States if you feel like it, but that's going to stay my room."

"I suppose you have a separate shelf for me in the refrigerator? And in the kitchen cupboards? I'm on a very strict diet."

We helped her move her boxes into her room. When we got finished with that, she gave us a weeny little grin and said, "I'd like to be alone for a while. Then I'll come out and visit, and we'll get acquainted."

I guess we just stared at her.

"Well? Didn't you notice I haven't even told you my name?"

"What is it?" I asked. She was like a scorpion, ugly but pretty; mean, but wonderful to watch.

"I didn't tell you for a reason."

"Yeah?"

"It *was* June Shapiro. It's June Shaw now. I didn't want to be a victim of anti-Semitism."

Dave slammed away to his part of the house, he would have punched her out if he could have, but I stayed around.

"You go to UCLA, then?"

"Of course."

"What's your major?"

"Philosophy. I'm a senior."

"Great."

"I transferred from Arizona State. I had to get away from my father. He abused me as a child. Often."

"That's tough."

The next morning, I looked around the kitchen for my loaf of bread, and put water on to boil for coffee. A dozen eggs were hard-boiling already, and about six raw onions had been chopped up and piled on the sink. My butter was missing. I saw where it was, melting in a saucepan. Three quarters of a pound of it!

"Hey!" I said.

No one answered.

"Hey! *Who took my butter?*"

A thudding sound came from somewhere.

A long time ago somebody had built a partition down the middle of the kitchen. It had a little alcove to fit a refrigerator in, but it was too small, so our refrigerator sat outside. The partition couldn't be torn down because there was an old-fashioned back porch on the other side of it, with a washtub from the Stone Age. Austen sometimes took his instant oatmeal into the little refrigerator alcove to eat, sitting on the floor with his legs crossed. He liked it in there.

The alcove shuddered. Sort of a repeat of the earthquake from yesterday. I went around to the back porch. June Shaw stood by the washtub, which she'd filled up with steamy water that reeked of ammonia. She wore a black bikini and hiking boots. She'd hooked her fingers over three or four wooden coat hangers and was pounding them as hard as she could against the sides of the tub.

Washing out coat hangers. Why not?

"Don't you want to keep it down, June? It's not even seven-thirty. People are trying to sleep."

Austen stormed out of his room, took a look at both of us, and stormed back to bed. June set her chin and went on banging.

I watched her for a minute. "If you're counting on waking up Dave, you're going to have to do more than that. He sleeps down-stairs, remember, and he sleeps pretty sound. Maybe you could shoot a cannon off outside his window."

She tossed her hair and doubled up on the pounding.

"What are you trying to do, anyway? Why don't you let them soak? How does a hanger get dirty in the first place?"

"I'm watching you watch my breasts. Men love breasts that move."

She had me. I turned my back to her and went to the kitchen, where my toast was burning and what used to be my butter was bubbling like mad and turning dark brown.

"Fuck it," I said. "Oh, fuck it." I headed to my room to get dressed and go out to Denny's for breakfast. Before I left, I heard her screaming. "What happened to my *ghee*! You turned the fire up under it. How *could* you?"

I had a day's work in front of me, sanding down the walls of a new restaurant, then painting on primer. I didn't need this shit.

That night when I came home the smell of curry was all through the house, and I knew where my butter had gone. I was dead beat. I grabbed my towel and headed to the bathroom for a shower. My hair was full of plaster dust, my nails were split, and my disposition was shot. I decided not to go back the next day. They'd already paid me in cash, eighty dollars for my eight hours, but the work was worth at least a couple of hundred. It was close to seven o'clock, and I was too damn tired to even think of doing anything but crashing. I splashed water in my face and took a look at myself in the mirror, my bloodshot eyes, the plaster dust in my nose that looked like coke. Life was too short to live like this.

When I turned around to get in the shower I spotted something on the tub. It looked like a little red mouse.

I picked it up by its string and dropped it into the toilet and thought of Botticelli's *Venus* and Manet's *Olympia*. Either the great artists had it wrong or I was meeting the wrong kind of woman. Then I thought of Millicent Landry dressed in white satin and those athletic little breasts like baseballs with erasers on them and heard myself grunt. I'd take a shower and forget the whole damn thing.

Feeling clean at least, I wandered on out to find Dave, who looked unusually content. "Try some egg curry. June made it. Not bad at all. With Indian dried fish and homemade onion chutney. She says you can have some if you want."

"Where is she?"

"Some yoga class. She really is pretty good at that stuff. She was practicing down on the patio outside my room this morning. Had some Indian ragas turned up pretty loud. I was going to tell her to turn them down, but when I got to the window I saw she was topless. So I let her go ahead."

"Did she see you watching?"

"Nah. I was a regular Peeping Tom."

"Don't count on it."

My stomach growled. Against my better judgment, I went prowling in the kitchen, found some steamed rice and scary yellow curry. Spooned in some chutney. Cracked open a beer.

"Tod? Do you want some grapes? Do you want some grapes? They're right here, son. They're already washed. Do you want some? Take a bite. Do you want one? Just answer me, yes or no. Tod? Tod? Do you want some grapes?"

"I don't think he wants any."

"How do you know? Did you take some kind of class in mind reading?"

"I think . . ."

"There's no way you could know what he wants or doesn't want."

"That's not true."

"Tod? Talk to me, son. See these grapes? See? I'm eating one right now. Mmm! Good! No seeds either. Nice and cold. Don't you want one just like me? Answer me, yes or no. Answer me, Tod."

"He's not *going* to answer you, can't you see that?"

"Shut up! Shut up."

"I'm only saying . . . he won't answer you. Or he already would have."

"Do you want to fight? Is that what you want? Do you want a fight from me?"

"I was just saying . . ."

"Do you think he can hear us? He can hear us, can't he? Because he moves his eyes to look at us. He can talk too. Does he talk when I'm not home?"

"I . . ."

"What does he say, then? What does he say?"

"He's barely three! Even before, he didn't make much sense."

"You didn't listen to him! You didn't pay attention! People ask me, no, I mean it, they're always asking me, how come you always spend time at the office? Isn't that *rough*, hanging out with your clients? But at least with athletes, you're with people who understand the concept of discipline. Who have a purpose. People who know what their job is."

"You're saying I don't do my job?"

"I don't have to say it. Nobody has to *say* it."

"It was an accident."

"When I'm gone, does he talk?"

"He hardly talked before. He was slow in talking. You know that."

"Now he'll never talk."

"It's only been three weeks! We don't know what's going to happen."

"What do you want, Angela? Do you want me to pretend that what happened *didn't* happen? It happened."

"I know that. I know it."

"All I ever wanted in my life was a son. I thought I'd never have one. When Linda divorced me, I thought I'd never have a son. Then I had one."

"*We* had one. *I* was the one who *had* the son."

"I had a son for a little less than three years."

"You still have him!"

"I wanted a son, to teach him what I know. Every man should be able to have at least that out of life."

"You still *have* him. We still have him."

"Why do you lie? I never pegged you for a liar. Live and learn. Angela? I'm talking to you!"

"You're talking to hear yourself!"

"I come home for lunch, and I ask my son a simple question, and . . ."

"Please!"

"A simple question! And he looks at me. He looks at me, Angela! And I don't know what to think. All I know is I get a call at the office one morning, and I drive home, and there's some guy working on my own son. I want to know where you *were*, Angela . . ."

"Please."

"You had to be some place. Talking on the phone? Taking a shower? Ordering groceries from Gelson's? Hassling Millicent? Doing your goddamn nails?"

"I don't know where I was. I've told you a hundred times. I don't remember where I was."

"I know where you weren't. That's the important thing. I know where you weren't. Don't you? Don't you? Don't you? Angela? And now you're crying again?"

"I was in the house. He got out some way, I don't know how. And he fell in the pool."

"That's right."

"I was in the house. I don't remember what I was doing."

"Angela?"

"You talk as if I wanted it to happen. Why would I want that? He's my son too, he's my child. I don't know what to do, anything more than what we've been doing. But I have to tell you one thing. One thing! If you keep doing this, you're going to lose both of us."

"*You?* You're not going anywhere, because where would you go? What would you do?"

"I'm asking you, please."

"I just want to know . . ."

"*That's enough.*"

"Angela?"

"*Please.*"

"I guess . . . I suppose I'd better be getting back to work."

"Fine. That's fine."

"Are you going to be needing anything? Should I pick up anything at the store on my way back?"

"No."

"Will you call me if you think of anything?"

"Yes."

"If Tod . . . if he says anything, will you call me?"

"Yes."

"I guess I'm going now. I'll be back around seven."

"Fine."

"I can be home earlier."

She didn't answer him. His steps clicked away on cement and she called after him softly, "What about the fence? You were the one who didn't want there to be a fence."

I waited until the Cadillac rolled out the drive, then I came out the back door from the kitchen. I was pretty sure Angela knew I'd been there. She sat at the patio table, shaded by the umbrella, holding Tod on her lap. One of his hands was tangled up in her hair. He was sweating.

"Is there something I can do?" I hated to see her look so sad.

"He doesn't know what he's saying."

"You tell me if there's anything I can do."

"I know what you can do. There's a bottle of wine in the refrigerator. And some fruit juice. Why not bring out a couple of glasses?" She leaned back and got the cricks out of her neck. Tod tightened his grip on her hair. Mary Cassatt, I thought. Too bad I can't paint like that.

When I came back with glasses and the bottles, Tod reached out to me. "Who," he said.

I took the kid. "That could mean *you*," I said.

"It could," she said, and smiled.

When Millicent came home a half hour later, she brought out another glass, and the three of us played around with Tod until some late afternoon fog chilled down the yard.

A day or two later, I was back in their laundry room wedged behind the dryer. Something about the wiring wasn't right. Man, my weak point. The washing machine was working OK, shaking this whole part of the house, smelling up the room with bleach, but the wiring behind the appliances was iffy and the dryer had quit. It was a real quiet morning, right around eleven o'clock. I'd been here since eight, working hard.

You have skin like peaches.

I focused on the pipes and wires just beside me, and I actually saw the place where the dryer had burned out. For once, it looked easy to fix. I wiggled out and sat up, brushing possible dust out of my hair, and trying not to sneeze.

"I need some duct tape."

"It's out in the garage, on the shelves to the right. Can I put this load in the dryer?"

"Yeah, but wait before you turn it on. I *think* I can get the wiring right by now." In four weeks, she'd figured out that half the time I didn't have a fucking clue what I was doing, and I didn't mind her knowing. How could I mind? Every day after I woke up and had my breakfast and took my run, I got in the car and came over here, and saved almost everybody else for the afternoon. If I ever thought about it, I dreaded that there wouldn't be any more work for me here, but every day another damn thing would be busted. A house like this was like a big machine, always breaking down.

"After that, I've got a Chinese scroll upstairs in the hall. The wind blew too hard last night and tore it about a third of the way through. And two of the drawers in Mr. Landry's bureau won't shut."

I gave the dryer my best shot, then stood by Angela as she hit the switches. It began to whirl and heat up, and I slid back behind the machine to watch for sparks or smoke. It looked like I'd actually fixed it.

"Did you say something before?"

"You've got dust in your hair."

The scroll had a pretty bad tear. We both carried it down the stairs and unrolled it on the dining-room table. I told her that I'd take it to a real restorer, but she said that they'd bought it for less than twenty dollars, so it wasn't worth it. I fished around in the "everything drawer" in the kitchen, found some wide Scotch tape, cut off four inches, taped it to the back of the scroll.

"Good as new. Maybe better."

But I hit a snag with Landry's stuck drawers. For a while I made them worse than they were, so that I couldn't pull them out at all and I couldn't push them back in. About that time, Tod woke up from his morning nap. He tiptoed up behind me, as I was stretched out along the floor, trying to look up and underneath to see how the drawer runners actually looked. The kid stuck both his hands in my hair. It seemed like that was his new thing to do. I yelled, with lots of false surprise. "Oh my *gosh*! What *is* that?"

Tod laughed like a maniac and ran from the bureau out into the middle of the bedroom to hide behind the bed.

He did it again.

And then he did it again.

"Tod, that's enough, honey. Let Bob do his work."

"I *want* to play," I said, and this time I caught the kid as he sneaked up behind me. "This beats working any day." I realized it was true. This wasn't how grown-up men were supposed to spend their time, but God, this was nice. Angela was wearing one of her long dresses and her hair was loose; she curled up on a chair in the corner of the bedroom and caught Tod every time he ran in her direction. For some reason I thought of Paris and that guy who worked in computers. He had the wrong idea. He was working too hard.

"You know," she said, "we could get out of here. We could—I don't know—we could take Tod to the zoo. It's Saturday. I'd buy your lunch. And," she added in a rush, "I'd pay you for your time, because you'd be baby-sitting."

"Sure thing," I said, and caught Tod as he threw himself down on my chest again and grabbed my hair. "I can't fix these drawers anyway."

Griffith Park was only fifteen minutes away from Hancock Park, but it seemed like a parallel universe, a different world. I had memories about that place that went as far back as when my mom and dad were still together. On Sundays, in the far past, I'd get scrubbed up and dressed in a short-sleeved shirt and baggy slacks and they'd take me out to see the bears (on the left side in the old zoo, as you climbed up the steep entrance slope) and the monkeys and elephants, and then cut out early to hit the pony rides. (I still had pictures of myself somewhere, looking nervous and a little bit geeky, holding on for dear life as my pony walked around the ring.) And then the train museum, where you could climb up and down on trains for a half hour or so, and then the merry-go-round, jammed right up against two green hills, just a great place.

But that was then. As we drove on into the park and I got ready to get lost—because didn't everybody get lost when they drove into Griffith Park?—it seemed like we'd turned off Los Feliz Boulevard straight into Mexico. The lawns, which I'd always remembered as more or less deserted, were packed with big family picnics, moms and dads and grannies and a million little kids. All the public barbecues were in use and a layer of smoke made a low roof over the whole scene.

"Let's get out of the car," Angela said. "Let's look around."

I had a moment's worry about gangs—Landry wouldn't be crazy about it if one of us came home with a gunshot wound, unless, of course, it was me—but I parked the van and we got out, and all of a sudden I felt a serious jolt of happiness. Life, outdoors, in LA. Families, kicking back. The smell of good food. Music coming in fragments from all over the huge ratty lawn. What could be better? I looked over at Angela and Tod. They both had the same smiles.

We ended up eating tacos from a vendor. Tod found a couple of little kids who were rolling a big ball back and forth in the shade under a tree. I wished I'd remembered to bring a blanket to sit on, but Angela had changed into Levi's, so we sat on the lawn and watched the kids roll the ball, catch it, laugh, look at us to make sure we were watching, laugh, send it out again, wait for it to be caught, catch it again, laugh again, look at us again, and so on. Maybe twenty feet away, on a big patchwork of blankets, some moms and aunts and grannies sat and smiled—at the kids, and at us.

Guys too. I saw two or three of the toughest-looking hombres in the world lying there, playing with their kids. And a fat guy in an undershirt lay on his back with his mouth open, snatching forty winks, with a fat little kid snuggled up under his arm, snoozing in exactly the same way. If I'd been drawing, it would have been great to do all of this, a park series, except no one would want it, or believe it.

But if I decided to use acrylic, I could do something really beautiful in an old-fashioned way, with the lawn's faded green, and the patchwork of old bedspreads, and that fat guy with his look-alike kid, and especially Tod with his big ball and his never-ending laughs.

I actually grunted out loud. Because no matter how good my draftsmanship and speed and technical skill, my taste was all in my mouth, as one of my professors had so kindly told me once. I didn't have a clue. Little kids on the grass! I'd end up painting on velvet if I didn't watch out.

But Angela heard me and misunderstood. "It's amazing, isn't it? And we luck into it like this." She sighed. "I want to thank you for coming with us. I wouldn't have had the nerve to come alone. Look at Tod. Look at him!"

Roll the ball, wait for it to be caught, catch it, laugh, look around to see who's watching, laugh like crazy, roll it out again. Sometimes it pays to be a little kid.

Because then he gets to sleep for a half hour, scooped up against his mom, while I forage across the lawn for soft drinks, and come back with three wet bottles of Peñafiel and three big straws.

The sitting ladies smiled at me as I came back.

"*Su hijo?*"

"Oh . . . *sí*," I said. "He's mine," and ducked my head nervously.

"*Qué bonito!*"

"*Gracias*," I said.

Later on, we drove up to the zoo itself. It was too late to go through the whole thing, but Angela thought she remembered a Children's Zoo that would be OK for Tod. It was hot, July hot, but not impossible. We walked up the slow incline, each holding on to one of Tod's hands.

"I used to come here," I said, "when my mom and dad were still together."

"My parents and I used to come here too." She didn't look very happy, so I said, "So, no bears? They used to be my favorite. And didn't they used to have just two broken-down seals?"

"Yes."

The Children's Zoo loomed up on our right, and we pushed through the turnstile. A bunch of baby goats, their heads on a level with Tod's, came up looking for food. I put some quarters in a machine, came out with kibble, and crouched down by the kid. "See? Put some in your hand, Tod. They'll come right up and eat." I stood back up and watched as the animals pushed and jockeyed for position as if they'd never seen food before. Tod shrieked with happiness and held his ground.

"You can't tell me he's not better," I said, but as I turned to look at Angela I saw she might be crying.

"So!" I said. "Were you any fun before all this stuff happened?"

"*Was* I? Before I got married, you mean? The life of the party. Dances and parties, my middle name!"

"I wish I'd known someone like you. All I ever wanted to do was be an artist, and I was a real pain about it, with my boring secret life, my *artiste* life."

"I never had any ambition. I just want, like what we have today. Like . . . that time in the day when nothing's happening. As if it were three in the afternoon, on a weekday. Or four. And everything's in order. You don't have to start dinner for a couple of hours. And you're out in the backyard. Or on the porch. And the kids are fooling around. Or one of your friends comes over. Just hanging out. On a lawn. Because, in my life, even though it's so ordinary, I can't seem to get to it."

"Here's how rare it is, Mrs. Landry. I never saw any of that except at your house, and I'm twenty-eight."

"*Where's Tod?*"

He was gone. We looked around the dusty enclosure. The goats, full of food, were dozing, sitting under a pepper tree. The chickens had taken shelter in a little open coop. A few bedraggled sheep looked at us without much interest. A baby llama chewed on some hay. At the far corner, a few humans clustered together and pointed at something.

I hotfooted it over there, feeling sick.

There was a pond, full of muddy water. Two calves knelt to drink, very picturesque. In the pond, Tod stood up to his waist, laughing, batting at the calves' faces with both his hands.

"Does anybody own this kid?" an old man in a baseball hat asked the crowd. He held on to a little girl with both hands. She looked as though she'd give a million bucks to hop in the water with Tod.

"Oh. Oh, God." Angela was standing next to me by now, both hands over her mouth.

I jumped in, scooped up the kid, sloshed out.

"Was it fun, buddy? Did you think it was time to cool off?"

I tried to keep smiling at the disapproving adults and envious kids, tried to stay mellow as a keeper in a uniform came over. "Is there anything wrong here?"

"Not a thing, took a dip to cool off, is all. Come on, Angela! We don't want to be late getting home!"

Walking back down the asphalt slope to the parking area, I took it upon myself to say, "Try and be cool. We don't want to upset him, he doesn't know what he did. You're going to be wetter than *he* is, if you don't stop crying!" And to the kid, I said, "So, *Tod*! Went for another swim, did you? What *is* it with you, boy? Was it the water you went for, or the cows?"

Tod held on to me with one hand and gestured expansively at the parking lot, the park, the whole world. "Saw a cow!" he said happily. "Saw a cow."

Two in the afternoon. Maybe three. Everything OK. Couldn't be better.

It inspired me to drive over to Atwater Village, after I'd dropped them off, to an art store with great prices. I stocked up on my favorite acrylics—Prussian Blue, Payne's Gray, Dioxazine Purple, Cadmium Red Extra Deep, and Phthalocyanine Green—too dark for me, maybe, but pure and translucent. He saw a cow, did he? Cadmium Yellow. Cad Yellow. Thal Green.

8

The bungalow sat back from the crumpled sidewalk on Manzanita, a few blocks down from the hill, baking in the sun. It had been painted white once, but that had to have been a long time ago. Another one of these sorry places I'd grown up with. I'd walked home from school along here. If Micheltorena was on the hill, Manzanita was in its valley, a shallow, disreputable street just north of Sunset where engineers must have been so at a loss about how to level the damn land that they gave the whole thing up and ended it in a staircase; you had to climb up on foot from here to the boulevard to do your shopping. Not that any of these people cared. Immigrants, senior citizens, bummed-out guys whose only social life had to be with their parole officers. Who around here had gotten it together enough to call a handyman?

White paint, on old, old wood bleached by the sun, splintered off by weather, and the brown wood underneath bleached to silver. That combination of white and silver looked good if you didn't think of the poverty that went with it. A slanting roof with asphalt tile, a front porch that went the width of the house, those pudgy columns of beach rock and concrete that builders used to like in California at the beginning of the century—and big, stringy hydrangeas on either side of uneven steps going up. Unmowed lawn, of course.

Ask for Hank, the phone message had said. The door opened and a tired-looking guy looked out. He was still probably in his twenties, wearing a black T-shirt, with an orchid tattooed on his arm. His hair was dyed matte black, but he looked strange—he looked like a hick. A bad smell came out around him.

"Hank?"

"Bob?"

"I'm the guy you called."

"Sure. Don't you remember me? Come in."

The shades were drawn in here. The windows were closed and the smell was worse.

"You do remember me? At that restaurant a couple of weeks ago? You had the machine and you were sandblasting the walls? That *under new management* deal? And out in the side yard, where some people were filling out applications, we got to talking when you were taking a break?"

"I guess I don't . . ."

"You said it was a good thing every day wasn't like this one, and I said, oh, you're not a painter then? Then you said *this isn't painting,* and you said you were a handyman. I said what do you do mostly, because, see, I already had a reason. And you said I do anything, anywhere, any time. So I asked you for your number, just in case. I didn't get that job, by the way."

The kid was a nervous wreck. What was going on here?

"What can I do for you?"

"I've got a friend here who's sick."

I got the picture right away, but I thought I might have it wrong. Weren't people with AIDS supposed to have it together by now, with Project Angel Food coming over every day with hot meals, and people dropping by to walk your dogs? Bringing you your AIDS cocktails?

Or so I'd heard.

"We rented this place about two months ago. We're here from Ohio. Southeast Ohio. It seemed like a good time to come. It's a good place to be out of."

Hank stood chatting with me in the hot dark room as if we'd known each other for years.

"Can I open a window?" I was afraid I might gag.

"Only out here, I think. The light hurts his eyes."

I pushed open the front door and lifted up a couple of windows. I remembered the furniture in here—I actually could identify some of it—as hotel issue from when I was a kid, moving from one furnished apartment to another with my folks. Painted stuff, stiff and off-balance, flaking. *Man!* That smell.

"We had a lot of fun for exactly one month before Ben got sick. I got my hair dyed and my ear pierced. We went to the beach. We'd never seen the ocean. It's different out here from Ohio. We went to readings up at A Different Light. It was like heaven, you can't imagine. To meet people like your own self. You know what we've got in Althea? The Tri-State Headquarters of the Klan. The Ku *Klux* Klan. Not a good place to be. Ben grew up in Carbonear, about thirty miles away. Do you know where we met? At a *church picnic* in Carbonear. They have a lot of survivalists out there, guys who hunt with crossbows, and both of us had been thinking for quite a while we were setting up to be targets. If there's anything they hate worse than an unfortunate nigger back there, it's a . . ."

"Hank? Is there something I can help you with here?"

Hank put down his invisible cocktail glass. Started to come to the point. "I think I bit off more than I could chew. I didn't know how sick Ben was, or even that he *was* sick. That's how dumb we were in Althea. He's just a kid. I shouldn't have taken him away from home. I brought him into a clinic one day a couple of weeks ago, but we can't *begin* to afford those drugs, and he doesn't have pneumonia, so they wouldn't admit him into a hospital. They treated him like he had AIDS, you know? Which he does, of course. They say he needs home care, but I don't know anything *about* it. Neither one of us has insurance. I worked with my brother-in-law back home. We had a delivery business. I don't know anything about taking care of people.

"Where is he?"

"Back here."

In what would ordinarily be the dining room, a thin little form stretched out on a twin-bed mattress. They'd covered up one window with foil to block out the light, but there was still enough light for me to catch the shine of urine and puke on the wood floor. Hank went on talking.

"I had to call somebody. Nurses are too expensive. I didn't know what to do." And, in a lower voice, "If I didn't call someone, I was afraid I might leave. Just walk out the door. I didn't know this would happen."

The kid turned his face toward us. It looked like the face had three eyes, and when I came closer, I saw that in a way it did. The kid was wearing a caste mark. His face was wet with sweat.

"How long has he been like this?"

"A couple of weeks, like I said. Maybe a little more. The hospital won't take him unless he has pneumonia, and he doesn't. He has a gastric upset. That's what they said."

"Do you have a washing machine here in the house?"

"No. The landlady's going to have a fit when she sees what he's done to her sheets. She only gave us two sets. We don't have much money, you know. I don't know what I can pay you."

"How are you, buddy?" I leaned over the kid so he could see me.

"I've been better." His voice was thin and shaky. He looked about thirteen.

"It's true you don't like the light?"

"Hurts my eyes."

I dodged out to the kitchen, rummaged around mostly empty cupboards and drawers, found a dish towel, doused it with cold tap water. "Put this across your eyes. I'll work around you."

I checked out Hank, in his jeans, black T-shirt, bad jewelry.

"You say you don't have any money?"

"If you're worried . . ."

"You must have enough to shop. I mean, while I strip the bed and get the laundry together, you walk up to the Junction and buy some food. Just go up the stairs at the end of the street. Jell-O, gin-ger ale. Chicken soup. Things for when you're sick. Have you called up Angel Food?"

"What's that?"

I rubbed my forehead. I didn't really know where to begin.

Hank got defensive. "We don't have a phone. We don't know anything about this place! We came into LA on a Greyhound off Highway 70 and took another bus out here from downtown. We got off at the wrong stop, we found out later. We got off at East Holly-wood when what we wanted was West Hollywood."

Ben gagged, moved his head off the bed, aiming for a pot on the floor beside him. Hit it, almost. The kid had nothing to throw up, but that didn't stop him.

"OK. Get going then. You do know where the grocery store is? Right there at the Junction? Walk two blocks, climb those stairs, turn left. It's across from the elementary school. Ginger ale and Clorox. Chicken noodle soup. I'll be working right here."

Once I was alone with the kid, I took a quick turn through the house. In the one bedroom, Hank's room, there was a bed, a few magazines on the floor, and a couple of posters on the wall, some guy on a motorcycle, another naked guy with a big dick. The high life! The kitchen was filled with empty cans and roaches and dirty dishes.

But the dining room was the big problem. And the bath. The kid had aimed for the toilet a few hundred times, but missed.

"Just lie there!" I called to him, not that he was going anywhere. "Don't move. I'll take care of everything."

I found a rag and some Comet in the bathroom, and splashed chemicals around on the basin, the toilet, the tub, the floor. I picked up dirty towels with the tips of my fingers and threw them into a pile in a corner of the dining room. But it was hopeless in here. Beyond thinking about.

I had a brainstorm. I went outside to the backyard, found a garden hose, poked it through the bathroom window, hosed down the entire cubicle, walls and all, for about ten minutes, as though I was washing a car. I'd give it time to dry and go in and scrub more later. If you broke the whole house down into six units—living room, Hank's room, bath, kitchen, Ben's room, *Ben*—one unit was slightly under control.

Five to go.

I headed around the side of the house to the kitchen, and opened all the windows. I smashed a few roaches and looked in the refrigerator. It was almost empty. So, you could say the kitchen wasn't as bad as the Walkers'! You just had to break it down into components.

I spotted a sad trickle of shit across the kitchen floor, grabbed the mop, found some 409 and some other junk. I cleaned it. I slammed some dishes through scalding water. I opened up the back door. Went outside, breathed fresh air.

I was there, outside, as Hank came in with a couple of sacks of groceries.

"I'll put those away," I told him. "You need to go back to the store. I think you need some of those—what do you call those things? Depends. And more Clorox. A couple more bottles."

Then I worked on the living room, putting off Ben until last. Nothing too bad out here. Nothing much to do. But bleak, *Jesus*! I mopped the hardwood floor and pushed the rickety tables and chairs into some kind of phoney order. But they needed a couple of extra chairs for the front porch, so the kid could get outside if he ever felt better.

"Are you having a nice time?"

"Huh?"

"Are you having a nice time?"

I went to the dining-room door and looked over at the kid. His head was thrown back, his eyes were hidden under the towel. The smell in here was, if anything, worse then ever.

"Are *you*?"

"Splendid," the kid said. "Splendid in every way. You troops have outdone yourselves."

His lips were horribly chapped and cracked. And where were his clothes?"

"Where are your clothes, uh, Ben?"

"When I get them too dirty, Hank throws them out. They really do get dirty. But I'm running out. Of my clothes. I never thought this would happen. My head feels like it's coming right off my body."

"How old are you, Ben?"

"Everyone asks me that."

"Well? How old are you?"

"How old are *you*?"

"Twenty-eight."

"I'm seventeen." The cracked lips smiled. "Just a child. A mere child. A youth."

"Stay there."

As if he were going anywhere.

I didn't know who else to call. I trotted out front, got my cell phone out of the van, and called up the Landry house. Millicent answered.

"I need some help, Millie. Some twin-bed sheets, two or three sets, and some double ones too. A pair of your dad's pajamas, two if you can get them, and about six old towels. Do you think you might have an extra rubber sheet around, left over from when Tod was a baby? As soon as you can do it. I'm over here on Manzanita north of Sunset by the Junction, about ten minutes away from you. By the staircase, do you know where that is? Can you do it right away? Tell your stepmom it's an emergency."

I waited on the porch until she drove up in that high school deb car of hers, a new Audi.

She was curious as hell. "Anything I can do?"

"No. I'll call you later. Thanks!"

I put clean towels in the bathroom and threw some more Comet around. Then I waited for Hank, who seemed to be taking a damn long time with those adult diapers. I walked around outside the bungalow, just breathing fresh air.

Hank came back with two boxes of Depends. "He's been lying there five days," he said hastily. "I have to tell you, maybe it's been more than a week."

I ignored him and walked back into the dining room. I took hold of Ben's forearm and gave him a little shake. "OK, kid, I'm going to change the sheets now. We're going to clean you up."

I pulled back the blanket and the top sheet. *Oh, God. Oh, Christ.* I stopped breathing and reached forward, grabbing Ben around the waist. "Can you stand up? Can you walk?" I marched the kid through the kitchen and called over my shoulder to Hank, "Come on! Come on out in the yard with us. Turn on the hose out back. Not too hard. Just steady."

In the backyard, I peeled off Ben's pajamas. They stuck to him in places, and when they came off, they left raw skin. I dropped them in a pile and stood bracing the naked kid. He shivered bluish-white in the hot sun, and kept his eyes closed. A tall rickety wood fence kept the neighbors from looking, as if they cared.

"Come on, Hank! Just turn the hose on both of us. Rinse us off. We'll give him a real shower later." Finally, I had to reach out and grab the hose from him. I turned it on myself first, straight down on the top of my head. The cool water felt great, and began to dent the smell.

"See what I'm doing, Ben? Take a look. Just rinsing off. It feels really good. Cover your eyes if the light hurts. Here goes." The water drifted down the kid's head in little rivers, and Ben tilted his face to it. He smiled, but his knees began to buckle. Hank rushed forward and grabbed him from the other side. I kept hold of the hose. I tried to think of it as an anatomy lesson, a memory from some long-gone UCLA art class. I pooled water in the hollows of the kid's collarbones and ran it down his chest and over his arms and lifted his arms to get under them. Brownish, reddish water pooled for a minute on the dry grass around him before it disappeared into the earth. I rinsed the kid's front; his little dick, his thin little thighs, his little kid feet. But when I took the hose around to the kid's back, I had to gag again. There was a pad of caked shit the size of a saucer in the center of his crack and up into the small of his back. And at the center of each cheek and at the point where his shoulder blades hit the sheets, there were four open sores. I kept pouring water gently, gently, over the sores, and over the pad of shit that shrank down and melted and finally disappeared.

I wanted to say something to that dyed and tattooed idiot Hank, but the guy had called someone, finally, and he hadn't run away. It would have been easy to do but he hadn't done it.

"Here's the deal," I said to both of them. "I'm getting a blanket and putting it down in the middle of the backyard. Ben's going to lie on his stomach and get some sun. I'm putting the mattress out in the sun and bringing out the old sheets. Hank, you're running the hose on them. Then I'll take them to the Laundromat."

They did what I said.

The dining room, once the sheets had been stripped, the bucket cleaned, the windows opened, the floor swabbed with Clorox, didn't smell so bad. I bundled together all the sheets and towels, put them in the van, got to the Laundromat run by two Hispanics up by the Junction. I shoved the loads in, got them washed and dried, and came home to find the two guys, one dressed, one naked, quiet and peaceful out on the back porch. Hank was sitting and Ben lying on his side, his head on Hank's thigh. Ben's hair was fluttering in the breeze, and Hank, looking dead beat, caught strands of it in his fingers. A long way from Althea.

"How're you feeling?" I put my hand on Ben's shoulder.

"Better. Splendid in every way," the kid said, and smiled a dreamy smile.

"Great. 'Cause now we're taking a real shower. Getting you really clean."

It turned out to be fun, in a crazy way. The three of us got soaking wet, half in, half out of the shower, trying to keep track of a cake of soap and a bottle of shampoo. Hank was probably relieved not to be preached at. Ben, with his dreamy smile, kept sticking his head straight into the warmish spray. Maybe he was so sick he didn't know any better. Maybe deranged. Or maybe both of them were just damn glad not to be alone. Who knew?

After the shower, I said Ben had to have another sunbath. Then—what about the sores? I didn't have fucking clue one. Minute by minute seemed to be the way to take it. I poured some

ginger ale for the kid to sip and found bottles of beer in the fridge
for Hank and me. The three of us sat on the back porch and drank.
Then we got Ben dressed in a Landry pajama top that hung on him
like socks on a rooster. The kid stood and let himself be dressed
with his eyes closed, looking happy.

"Do you want to go back to bed now?"

"For a while."

We took him back, made up the bed, put him down on his stomach, spread a sheet lightly over him, and then went back outside
with another couple of beers.

"You've got to do some stuff," I said.

"I know. But what? We don't know anyone. I'm afraid to leave
him alone."

"I'll make some calls. Get you some help. How much money do
you have?"

Hank reached into his pocket.

"*No!* I mean for doctors or food. Or calling home."

"Oh. Enough, I guess. For a couple more months."

"What do you want to do? What are you *going* to do?"

"I don't know."

I went out to the van again for my phone and called AIDS Project LA and Project Angel Food—the only two places I knew about.
I drove back to the store and got another six pack, a couple of hamburgers, a half gallon of milk. Then Hank and I sat down on the
back porch.

I told him about my calls. "They'll send someone by tomorrow,
if they can. I'm going now. I'll drop by tomorrow afternoon. Listen.
Hank?"

"Yeah?"

"Those diapers. You've got to put them on him. Don't let it get
like it was. But you're the one to do it. Not me. And be sure
he keeps drinking some ginger ale. He's probably dehydrated. If he
gets worse, call 911. *Make* them do something."

"All right. All right."

"OK, then, I'm going to see you both tomorrow, in the afternoon."

I tiptoed through the house, past the kid who was sleeping now, drawing long shivery breaths.

"Does he like to look at anything special? I could paint him something, maybe. A picture." The little room looked like a sorry jail.

"I owe you money."

"Not for today."

"I don't like to see you leave."

"You know my number. I'll be back, tomorrow, after my other work."

I drove off thinking I was OK, until my whole body seized up in a sob. I held on to the steering wheel and cried. When I got home I went straight to the shower and used up all the hot water. Then I got paranoid about possible holes in my skin and poured peroxide over my hands. I finally got a grip, more or less, and went out to the dining room where Dave sat, predictably, with a beer and a joint and an open book.

"I saw, ah . . . I saw an AIDS case today. A bad one."

Dave shook his head. Looked out the window. What was there to say?

I picked up a deck of cards, peeled out a game of solitaire.

Austen slouched into the kitchen, opened up some cereal, and looked into the room where we were. His eyes were bloodshot, his expression all spacey.

"Don't you guys ever work?"

"Lay off, Austen," Dave said. "Bob's been out all day with an AIDS guy."

But Austen couldn't come around. "Sor-*eee!*" he said, "How was *I* to know?"

I looked up from my cards. "You don't," I said, echoing the

thought pattern that had zoomed in and around my head for the last eight or ten hours, "have fucking clue one. About any of it. About anything. Not fucking clue one. OK?"

"Sor-*eee*," Austen repeated, into the silence. "Well, I'll go back to studying, then."

"Do that," I said, and put my hands over my eyes. "He had sores. Where he'd been lying there. No one to help him."

"Sorry," Austen said again, as he went back to his room. "Sorry."

CHAPTER

9

"You baaastaaard! I'll kill you, Hugh! Eeeee!"

Ten in the morning, in the Los Feliz hills. Against my better judgment, I'd answered another call from the Walkers. What *was* it with these people? I eyeballed the lawn and saw it had to be mowed again, probably hadn't been cut since the last time I'd been here.

The double-garage door was open and Samantha stood there, holding her arms straight out. She looked like she'd been crucified by invisible forces, and of course she was screaming to beat the band. Hugh stood close but not too close to her, grinning sheepishly. He gave me a feeble wave.

"What now?" I asked.

Hugh shrugged. "I don't know."

"He killed my guinea pig! He *killed* her! Oh, Guinea, Guinea, *Guinea!*"

I looked down at a cage on the garage floor. The guinea pig was dead all right. It had been eating a piece of navy-blue flannel, and lay on its side with a mouth full of flannel and a puffed-up stomach. It looked smug and self-satisfied, and dead as a box of marbles.

"Who gave him the cloth?"

"He did! He did! *Heeee* did!" Samantha came at Hugh, her fists going like crazy machines. He backed off, snickering, dodging her blows.

"My God. You kids. Well, before we do anything else we better have a funeral. Where's your mother?"

The kids exchanged a glance.

"Upstairs. She said we were driving her nuts." Samantha sounded like she thought the charge was unjust.

"I can't imagine why," I said. "Is that your ambition? To drive your mother into the nuthouse, and you only have this summer to do it?"

Now they both shrugged, and looked around.

"Let's go. Somebody find a shovel. We'll go out back."

"We're too old for funerals," Samantha told me. "You bury him. We'll wait here." She seemed pretty queenly about it.

"Too old for funerals but not too old to sound like an air-raid siren?"

"*Yeah,*" Hugh added, and Samantha lunged at him again.

"How's the snake?" I asked, as I poked around the garage for a shovel, and they both answered together, "Oh, fine."

"I've got an aquarium now," Hugh said. "Lots of stuff. Some very good fish."

"Mom got this *turkey,*" Samantha whispered. "She's weird."

The funeral turned out to be pretty good. We put the guinea pig in a shoe box and lit some sparklers they'd bought for the Fourth of July. Mrs. Walker came out to watch, clutching her head. "I've got a terrible migraine," she moaned. "I can't take this much longer. These kids are driving me mad. I can't be expected to do all this alone."

Hugh and Samantha looked at her with concern, but neither of them seemed particularly inclined to change their ways.

"Where's Mr. Walker?"

"Playing golf in Hawaii. With clients. I didn't want to go. I *hate* those stupid businessmen in their stupid madras shorts. Besides, what would I do with Hugh and Samantha? I can't take *them* anyplace!"

"Ah, Ma," Hugh said.

"They both have ADD, did I tell you that? Both of them. Attention Deficit Disorder. Can you imagine? They can't pay attention."

I didn't know what to say to that. "What do you want me to do around here?"

"The turkey needs a pen. He makes a terrible mess. I don't know what I was thinking. I wanted a peacock, but the man told me they make too much noise."

"Did you ever think of a dog? No offense. But a dog, like other people have?"

Mrs. Walker waved over at Hugh and Samantha. "They're allergic. To *everything.* House dust, pollen, tree bark, tobacco. Especially dog hair. We can't have anything with fur."

I thought of the crud I'd seen in the Walker house, the dust to end all dust, but I didn't say anything.

"I've done everything I can," Mrs. Walker said. "No one can say I haven't done everything I *can.*"

Mrs. Walker was dressed today in beige linen slacks, a silk blouse, and white sandals with high heels. She looked great. For what? I got the momentary sinking feeling it might be for me. The four of us stood out back in the summer morning by the guinea pig's grave. The backyard was run down, but not out of control the way it had been two weeks ago. I flashed on Rudyard Kipling, *The Jungle Book,* and my brain took a hike. She could be a memsahib out in India somewhere. We could have been burying a mongoose, not a guinea pig. And time would be stretching out in front of all of us with nothing to do ever except wait until midnight when, if we were lucky, one of us might get to see the elephants dance. Why not? That's probably what some family was actually doing over in India right now.

"OK," I said. "Where do you want this pen? Hugh, why don't you come with me to the lumberyard? Mrs. Walker, are you going to be getting any more . . . fowl, or will this be for just one turkey?"

We decided on a place near the back of the yard, near a wall of dying, decrepit ivy.

"I just want my children to have everything a normal American family has," Mrs. Walker said. She did look especially cool in all her silk this morning, but wacky. "Pets and books and music and lessons. But because of their ADD all of it rolls right off them."

Hugh and I worked for most of the morning on the turkey pen. When it was finished, it looked solid and good. We'd both taken off our shirts and Hugh's back showed some sunburn. He seemed like an OK kid.

"Now that it's done, we've got one other thing to do," I said. I liked the look of the pen, I felt kind of dumb that I liked it, but I did. It felt good to know I could put something like that together.

Hugh shot me a grin. "I know. Catch the turkey."

For the next hour, the four of us chased the turkey around the yard. Mrs. Walker changed out of her silk into brief shorts and a halter top. Looking pretty good.

The turkey didn't want to get caught, but it finally got tired of the screams and the chasing and allowed me to fall on it. I grabbed its feet, turned it upside down, and heaved it into the pen. Samantha and her mother decided to get affectionate.

"Oh, *look* at it! A turkey in a *pen*. Turkey. Turk*eee*!"

I rolled my eyes. You couldn't hate these people. I almost liked them. And that right there was about as stupid as putting a turkey into a pen.

I went in the kitchen for a glass of water and was standing by the sink holding the icy glass against my forehead when Hugh came tearing past with Samantha right in front of him, running hard. "You *bitch*," he screamed at his sister. "I'll kill you. I'll *do* it this time!"

Hugh caught hold of her T-shirt, yanked her around to face him, pulled back his right arm, and clipped her square on the jaw. He knocked her out cold. Mrs. Walker came in from out back, took it all in.

"What *now*?" she shrieked. "What have you *done*?"

"She turned up the heater on my fish! They're dead, all of them. She *boiled* them to death."

Mrs. Walker didn't take it too well. "No!" she wailed. "*Noooo!* I can't stand any more of this."

Samantha opened her eyes and looked at her brother. She must have figured she was safe on the floor. "*You* were the one who put the flannel in the cage. You killed him."

Hugh was going to kick her, but I pulled him back.

"Hey! Cut it out. We'll clean the aquarium and go get some more fish. Do you have one of those nets around?"

Poor old Hugh seemed fully crushed. He watched as I skimmed what seemed like a thousand poached bodies off the top of the water, and scraped tears off his cheeks. I tried to get his mind off it.

"Do you know the phone number of the place where you got all this stuff? Why don't you call them and see if there's anything we can do, or if we have to change all the water or what? Maybe we can go on over and stock up again right away. Go ahead, do it, Hugh."

The temperature of the water was already going down and the filter seemed to be working OK. I put my face close up to the glass and began going over every inch of the aquarium, trying to find any more dead bodies. Just a couple left, down at the bottom.

When Hugh came back, he looked a little better. "They say . . . it will probably be OK. And we can go over there right now."

The two of us drove to a fish store on Melrose. The quiet in the van was a relief, and Hugh seemed glad to be going out again on a guy's errand with a guy.

"So, Hugh. I don't want to butt in, but what *is* it with you guys?"

"What do you mean?"

"Jeez, Hugh! You're always trying to massacre your sister, that's what I mean. Or she's always trying to massacre you. Can't you, uh, go to camp or something? Now that it's summer?"

"Got to stay home with Mom."

"Maybe she'd like some peace for a change."

"Can't do it."

"But . . . what's the deal here? I don't know how to tell you, but most of the world doesn't carry on the way you guys do."

Hugh shrugged his shoulders. "So?"

"No, I mean it. It's not good for you. I mean, think of the fish. This morning they were happy fish. Now they're in fish heaven. Think of the guinea pig . . ."

"I hate that stupid pig!"

"So, Hugh. What grade are you in?"

"Seventh. Eighth next year."

"What school?"

"Thomas Starr King."

"I went there when I was your age."

Hugh shrugged again.

"Couldn't you go over and see some friends? Spend some time away from the women?"

"I told you. We've got to stay home with Mom."

"Who says?"

Hugh shrugged.

"What?" I asked. "What?"

"If we went away, she'd be alone."

"So? A lot of women stay in a house by themselves. Or maybe she could go out—do whatever they do. Play bridge or something. Get her hair done. Have lunch with a friend."

"She hates that stuff. Besides, she doesn't have a taco."

"I'm sorry?"

"A taco. On her combination plate. That's what Dad says."

"And that's why he's never around?"

Hugh looked worried. "He's around."

"What about this taco?"

"Like floors missing in her elevator shaft? That kind of stuff."

"Your mom seems OK to me. A little high-strung, maybe. At least she hasn't murdered any animals today."

We were on Melrose now, and I kept an eye out, looking for a parking place.

"She doesn't come from out here."

"What?"

"She doesn't *come* from out here."

"You could have people over. Your own friends."

"To my house? Yeah, right."

The fish store was air-conditioned and cool. My mind kept wandering. Like, here were these watery worlds rising up on every side of me, closed universes where fish didn't yell at each other and no fish was alone and no fish had to choose a meaningful career. Nobody bothered them, and they didn't bother anybody.

The clerk found a computerized list of all the fish in the Walker inventory and boxed up an army of specimens, all in white cartons, like a big Chinese dinner. He was in a pretty good mood. The store was making solid money off this. "Say. Want an iguana? I'll throw in an iguana for another twenty bucks. Just came in this morning. Full grown. Shouldn't really be here. Got to get him off my hands. They're easy to take care of. Put him in an aquarium with some gravel on the bottom. Feed him flies. Maybe hamburger. Nice bright green. No allergy problems."

I wondered how many kids had been taken by Westside parents to allergists for those tests, and now they could never own a puppy again. Which probably accounted for the thousands of homeless pets all over the city. Which accounted for all the Westside animal rights activists.

"Can I?"

"Can you what?"

"Have the iguana?"

"Why not? Pick up another aquarium for it. Your mom probably won't mind. It's all going on her card."

We didn't talk much on the way back. I could feel the presence of the iguana on the seat behind me. He wasn't in a good mood.

Of course, when we got back to the house and unloaded the fish, and I told Samantha to keep her hands off the aquarium thermostat from now on, and then let her open some of the cartons to let the fish fall in, she was the one who opened the one with the iguana in it.

"It got *awaay*!"

The iguana zoomed out the back door and scrambled out across the lawn—avoiding the ivy, thank God. It ran up the trunk of a large sycamore tree, where it settled down, and got into the groove of pretending to be a set of green leaves.

"OK," I said, "all right." I was getting tired of this. "Someone get me the ladder."

From then on, I decided to consider the afternoon as a study of color and almost-still life, something I'd be putting in my portfolio for Otis; the silver brown of the tree trunk, the midsummer green of the leaves—Thal Green?—the entirely different green of the iguana, who seemed to have quite the personality, now that I was getting to know him.

Even though it was July, a trick in the Los Feliz hills seemed to make the sun go down early, and the colors got a lot deeper as the direct light disappeared. It was beautiful up in the tree. It looked to me a lot like the insides of those aquariums—leaves brushing against each other, the tickle of the iguana's claws against tree bark that I could barely hear. The yelling down on the grass faded away. If they were going to keep on making that racket, they'd have to do it in their own world. I was out of it now.

"You going to make it easy for me? Or are you going to make it hard?"

The iguana ignored me. He was snippy beyond words.

I settled in.

Mrs. Walker and the kids got bored and went inside.

The afternoon darkened down.

The iguana kept an eye on me. Then it seemed like it didn't keep an eye on me. That it might be thinking of something else.

About a half an hour after that, I snapped out an arm and grabbed the thing behind his head.

"Two can play," I told him. "Two can play your game."

The iguana had a fit but I held on like death as I skinned down the ladder, trotted across the lawn, and banged on the back door with my free hand.

"Open up! Samantha! Hugh! Be ready to give him something to eat."

In the kitchen, once they got the iguana put away, they treated me like a hero. It was out of the question for me to go home, Mrs. Walker said. I had to let them take me to dinner. Why not? I didn't have anyplace else to go. I stood in the kitchen under bright lights drinking a gin-and-tonic Samantha had made for me, and listened to them discuss the pros and cons of where to eat: Chan Dara? No, it was bound to be too crowded by this time of night, and besides, Hugh was sick of Thai food. Anywhere Italian? No! Too hot for it. Spicy food is good for you in hot weather, Hugh said, but the women overruled him. Italian food isn't *spicy*, Hugh, it's just rich! Well, well . . . what about Mexican food down at Barragans on Sunset? But Mrs. Walker thought the neighborhood was too iffy after dark. What about that Caribbean place, Cha Cha Cha?

"I'm getting faint," I said, but drunk was more like it—the gin hit my empty stomach pretty hard. "Is there a Tony Roma's around here? Don't ribs sound good?"

The restaurant glowed like a darkroom. We turned out to have a great time, gnawing on corncobs and spareribs and acting dumb. Hugh and Samantha built stockpiles of ribs by their plates and before dinner was done they began lobbing them sneakily at each other. Their mother told them to cut it out, but then stockpiled a few of her own. I thought it might be a good idea to do the same.

After the waitress had brought us second rounds of g-and-ts, I watched Hugh as he aimed for his little sister, and just as Hugh threw, I threw at Hugh, catching the kid above the ear, right by his hairline.

"*Yow!*" Hugh yelled so loud that the noise in the restaurant stopped for a minute and people at other tables began to look around in the dark to see who had caused the commotion.

The four of us stared down at our plates.

"*You* did it," Hugh whispered to me.

I did my best to look pained. "You did it, Hugh. I saw you. Picking on your sister like that. It's a disgrace. Mrs. Walker, I don't see how you put up with these little bandits."

She leaned back and gazed at them fondly, a shiny layer of grease at the corners of her lips. "They're completely out of control," she said. "The bane of my existence." Then, to the waitress, "We'll be taking these bones home. I'm making soup stock."

Back at the house I came in for one last drink, and the bones from the doggy bag began to fly. It went on for almost an hour. Finally, the Walker family ganged up on me and pelted me with bones which I grabbed and put away in my own stockpile until they all ran out. I got to my feet and threw up my hands. "I surrender!"

"What are you going to do with those bones?" Samantha asked suspiciously.

"Bury them?" I suggested.

"Out by the guinea pig?" Hugh blurted out, and then fell over, crippled with laughing. He thought he was the funniest thing in the world.

Even Samantha laughed.

"What we could do is make a ring of bones around the grave, like Stonehenge. I could come by tomorrow afternoon. We could do it together."

"Now it's time for bed," Mrs. Walker said. "Go on. You know it is."

Samantha hugged her mom and then hugged me. "Tonight was *fun*," she said. "You're coming back tomorrow then?" Her broad face was blissed out. She was a sweet little kid.

"Sure. After work. We'll stick in those bones. Maybe I'll paint some of them."

Hugh waved and disappeared upstairs. Right on the edge of being a cool dude. Samantha went after him.

"You know," Mrs. Walker said, "I just remembered. I never did put feed in for the turkey. He has water in his pen but no feed. Would you go out with me to put some in? I get a little nervous in the dark."

She didn't look nervous. She didn't look nervous at all. All the laughing, and certainly the gin, had loosened up the muscles in her neck and along her jaw. Her hair was a thick natural blonde with some silver in it, and it gleamed in the yellow light.

"Can we have another drink?"

She nodded again, and mixed us a couple of strong ones. We sipped on them as we wandered through the garage, found a plastic bucket, loaded up on feed, and went on out across the lawn.

It was dry as Africa. I kept thinking of the iguana in the tree, and that luminous, concentrated green. How many iguanas had escaped from how many cages in this city? How many reptiles were out there tonight in magnolias and sycamores and jacarandas? What if this were a jungle pretending to be a city? I'd had a lot to drink.

Something rustled out in the ivy. "You ought to let me cut some of this back," I muttered, and I was surprised at how throaty my voice sounded. I groped for the pen's fence, found it, and pitched in the bucket of feed. The turkey was asleep for the night, but he gave a reflexive gobble.

Mrs. Walker took my hand and pulled me behind the pen, right up against the ivy. I couldn't say I was surprised; I'd been considering the possibility all night. Would I draw the line at a woman who could be almost forty? Hell, no! Why should I draw the line? She was squirmy and pretty and jittery and vague and drunk. Her lips went all over my face like she was a pony looking for a sugar cube, and I just stood there, letting her do it. She shucked off my shirt and took off her blouse and then her skirt. Her arms went all over me like a spider monkey. She had a surprising amount of energy. I got out of my jeans and next thing I knew I was flat on my back in the dry grass. I put up one of my hands to touch her breasts, but she pushed it away. "Stay still!" she told me, and I did, still as the iguana had been in the tree, keeping from coming by imagining Hugh or Samantha snooping out across the lawn. I concentrated on the dusty smell of the ivy and the lawn and the jungle smell of Mrs. Walker, and the breathing sounds of the snoozing turkey and the husky breath of Mrs. Walker, and the amazing circular feeling of being screwed right into the baked dirt of the Los Feliz hills.

When she finished—which I had to notice, because her whole body went rigid as a crossbow, I allowed myself to come and cursed myself for not having brought a condom with me. But who could have known I'd get lucky *here*? She slid right off me and sat in the grass.

"I miss it so much."

"Is he gone a lot? I guess he is, huh?"

"Not him! Yes, he's gone a lot, but I miss . . . staying up late, until . . ."

"I have to go home now," I whispered. "I can't play anymore."

"Oh, you!" She rapped at my chest with her fingernails. "This isn't even what I was talking about. This was nice, but I mean those *real* nights. Now that I'm married, I'll never have those real nights again."

"What about your husband?"

"He's all right. He's a schmuck, actually. I can't stand him."

"No, I mean . . ."

"Robert, I couldn't pick him out of a lineup. He's a bleb."

"Isn't there something you could do?"

"There's nothing else I want to do. So there's no point leaving him. Or kicking him out." The change in her voice told me she'd given it some thought. "Besides, what would I do then? I don't want to work, it's a waste of time. I like staying home with the kids."

The kids. I suddenly saw myself, buck naked, flat on the grass between a wall of ivy and a turkey pen with their mom. The thought, which should have shrunk me down to nothing, worked the other way. I reached for her, but she pinned me back to the grass.

"Wait! Stay still. Let me get on."

"You're all romance," I said.

She didn't bother to answer.

I concentrated again on breathing, making it last, inhaling dust and the smell of sweat. I was still pretty drunk and that made me think I could see things the way the iguana saw them. It seemed very important—to be able to live in a separate world, up in a Thal-Green tree, perfectly quiet in a world of leaves and breeze and elegance of air.

"The one place I always wanted to go was Calcutta. Doesn't that seem splendid in every way?"

Ben was better now, but you could see he was still weak. He got up sometimes to sunbathe in the backyard, but he didn't like to go out in public. He stayed in the dining room on his bed and watched people move around him, and he was hardly ever alone; Hank stayed with him.

"Why Calcutta? You talk about it all the time." I'd done a little straightening up around the house and was spelling Hank so he could go for a walk. I had a surprise in mind for later, and I asked the kid again, "Why Calcutta?" But Ben had dozed off.

In the three weeks I'd known these guys, I'd changed my mind about Hank. The guy had a lot of courage. Courage to come out to LA to live the life he'd always wanted, but more courage to have stayed in that Ohio town for the whole first part of his life, living with his Christian parents, impersonating a tough guy when he drove trucks for his brother-in-law, fending off country girls who— over the years—had thought he was "cute."

And I couldn't even measure Ben's courage.

Every afternoon, I tried to come by. Every afternoon when Hank got back from his walk, we'd pull a couple of beers out of the refrigerator. The two of us would sit on the front porch, just a couple of guys in Levi's and T-shirts, chugging our brewskies and watching the life of this little street, Chicana girls pushing babies in strollers, old, forgotten white ladies who hadn't moved out after their husbands died, and a lot of young guys washing their cars. Hank would tell me what it was like talking to strangers on the phone about their setup. He told stories of missed appointments and lost papers and counselors at AIDS Project Los Angeles, who started out sounding like they could do something but got less and less enthusiastic when they heard the whole story—that he and Ben were from out of state, that they didn't have insurance, that neither of them had job benefits, or family, or money, or even a car.

Then he'd change the subject, and it turned out he was homesick. He talked about what it was like back home—the American plainness of it—miles of woods and grassland and scrubby hills that never got anywhere and that hadn't changed since the whites took the land from the Indians. The one-street town of Althea, all built of red brick. The truck-driving school they had there, where guys who couldn't read or write learned to drive semis as big as a football field, and what *bad* drivers those guys were! The strip joints outside of town, where you watched girls you'd gone to high school with take off their clothes.

The churches. Hank had been raised a Methodist, and he would say, even now, that he believed in God. The best thing about the church had been piling into buses and going out in youth groups and young adult groups to meet youths and young adults in other towns, which is how he'd met Ben. Carbonear was famous for its all-day picnics. Every town back there had those all-day picnics, because none of them had movie theaters; you had to drive ninety miles to Columbus to see a flick, so it was better to pile into a church bus on a Saturday morning in the spring and head out to Carbonear or somewhere else and sit down on a curb in the sun and watch hours of barbershop quartets and banjo players and funny-looking girls in homemade costumes doing clog dancing. Later, they'd all go over to some church basement, or out to a meadow full of ticks, and eat chicken and potato salad and apple pie and Cool Whip and then go home. Singing sometimes, as the bus drove dark roads in the night.

A couple of days ago, Hank had said, "I thought, if I even thought about it at all, that my whole life was going to be that way, a big lie, a tragedy. But one Saturday I took my eyes off the banjo players and there was this beautiful boy, just a kid, sitting on the curb a few feet away from me, leaning back against a streetlight in the sun. He said, 'I'd rather be in Calcutta, wouldn't you? Or out with General MacArthur's troops in Corregidor?' And I thought, my God, maybe there *is* a God. He said, 'Would you like to go down and take a walk by the river?' Just like that. We both got up and left the street and the people and walked a couple of blocks over to the river that goes through that town. We slid down the mud banks until we got to the water and walked for about a mile up to where it looked like the Indians might still be living. Then we had sex. I was a virgin up until then. But Ben wasn't."

I listened, and thought about my poor mom. Or my dad. Or myself, is more like it. Or poor everyone. Waiting around in life watching the equivalent of bad clog dancing, and maybe there would never be the person who would catch your eye and say *I'd rather be in Calcutta,* or whatever words it took to wake you from your sleep.

"I'd been saving all the money I ever made because I still lived at home. God knows I never went out on dates or bought clothes, or even took a drink. The fourth week we were together, I asked Ben if he wanted to go out west. We thought of San Francisco, but Ben said he wanted heat and squalor. Something as far away from Carbonear as possible. We got it! We got the squalor part right. We got the heat too."

Today I'd brought my paints, and one of my new stretched canvases. I'd had the thought to paint Ben, in "Calcutta." The drawing itself was pretty much in place. I worried now about the feelings, and the color. The trick would be to get the pure blond Ohio part of the kid, together with the India of his dreams. And give Ben something good to look at from his bed.

I set up my easel and chair in the dining room and began to lay on paint. I laid out pale Ben, just as he was, flat and thin on his single bed. I painted in his caste mark. Amethyst. I got the perfect color of his almost-white hair against the faded turquoise sheets the Landrys must have had for a long time before Millicent nabbed them.

All around the bed, I'd sketched in my idea of India. Luscious curling vines with monkeys in them, and more monkeys eating mangoes. In the foreground, I painted in blocks of children, naked and ghostlike, beautiful beggars, standing next to each other in crowded streets. But I gave them all handfuls of gold coins. I put coins in all across the bottom of the canvas, and didn't hold back on the glitter. Above Ben, I'd drawn in some kind of god. I knew zip about Indian religion but I painted a handsome prince and made him look a lot like Hank, with black hair and a tattoo. The prince would be dressed in purple silk, every finger of his hands covered with jeweled rings. And he'd send out rays of golden light. The light and coins would circle around the sleeping boy in a shining haze.

Ben had drifted off to sleep again and I thought some more

about the picture. After a while, I mixed up two or three shades of deep lilac. I painted over the caste mark in the picture, changing the amethyst spot into a perfect vanda orchid. (They always said I was a good craftsman.) Then, using the same brushes, I painted an orchid over the caste mark on Ben's own forehead.

I worked very fast on the Indian jungle and the naked children, and as the sun began to go down, I cleaned up my paints and folded my easel, and propped the painting against a far wall. An Angel Food volunteer came by—a stout little woman with cartons of pureed vegetables and carrot juice. I took her into Ben's room to check out the work.

"Amazing!" she whispered. "You've made them both into saints from heaven."

When Hank came back, winded and sweaty from his walk, he covered his mouth with his hand. "You saw what made me fall in love with him. You have a gift, you know that?"

We lit a bedside lamp and waited for Ben to wake up. When he did, we propped up the painting at the bottom of the bed so he could see it. "I love it," he said. "It's so beautiful. It's the most beautiful thing I've ever seen."

"Now, look at this," I said. I found a hand mirror and held it so that he could see the orchid on his own forehead.

"Oh, I love it. Oh, it's splendid in every way."

"Bob, we need you!"

"Yeah, who is it?" The sun was barely up but already my room was stifling. The air was so thick you could gag on it.

"It's his birthday, and he's going to be home for once." She giggled, and I recognized the lunacy. Mrs. Walker.

"How's the menagerie?" I asked groggily.

"Oh, Bob. The menagerie's OK. You were a big help last time."

"How do I answer that one?"

"Oh, Bob! What I mean is, Michael actually said a few nice things when he came home last time. He said he almost thought I might be getting my act together. I guess . . . we might be really trying again."

I pulled myself up to a sitting position, and kicked off the sheet. A stone July scorcher coming up. "That's nice," I said.

"So it's Michael's birthday a week from today on the twenty-

sixth, and I thought I'd give him a party. Seven hundred of his clos-
est friends."

I had to laugh in spite of myself. "You want me to come over and
scrape the slime off the floor? You want me to paint the snake?"

She sounded almost prim in the way she chose to ignore me.
Like I was a bad little kid who'd forgotten my manners.

"We'll have to have it outside, of course. A garden party. I'm
renting a tent and a dance floor. And I'm calling the caterers today.
But we need some *decor*. And we'll need extra people for passing
hors d'oeuvres. The caterers want twenty-eight dollars an hour for
each extra person they bring. Don't you live with some people?
Couldn't they help out? And didn't you say you were a regular
artist? Didn't I hear you say that? Couldn't you whip me up some
decorations?"

"Ten dollars an hour. For my friends, too. How are Hugh and
Samantha?"

"They like the idea of a party. Can you come over this morning?
We've only got a week. Did I tell you that?"

"Have you sent out invitations?"

"Telegrams. Three hundred of them. Hugh's doing it today.
With the Rolodex."

"How's the laundry situation? How about your dishes?"

"Oh, *Bob*!"

I hung up, got up, went down the hall. Dave was already awake.
He hunched over the funnies and brushed powdered sugar off his
chin. A package of doughnuts lay open and I grabbed one.

"Want to pass some hors d'oeuvres next weekend? Wear a snap-
on bow tie? Ten bucks an hour."

"Sure!"

Even in the awful sun, a party seemed like a good idea, until I
drove up and saw the Walker house again, which still looked deso-
late and peculiar on this street with all its manicured respectability.

I went around to the back. At least nobody was screaming, but they might have been past the point of screaming. The three of them, Mrs. Walker, Hugh, and Samantha, stood outside in the sun, looking at the yard. Lawn needed mowing, of course. But the whole place looked raggedy-assed. All in all, beyond help.

Samantha ran over and hugged me. Hugh gave me one of his careful waves and a self-conscious smile.

"We're giving a party!" Samantha said.

"Cool! So what are you going to do out here?"

Mrs. Walker took a couple of deep breaths. She wore Levi's shorts and a flimsy white blouse, and she'd been lying out in the sun a lot. She looked good. "Fix it!" she said brightly. "You can do that, Bob!"

I don't know why, something about these people cheered me up. *"No problema,"* I said.

I drove down Sunset and over to St. Francis of Assisi Catholic Church, found the pastor, and asked if he had some parishioners of good character to do seven days of intensive gardening. Ten dollars an hour. After only fifteen minutes, I drove back with Lorenzo and Martin, shy young guys who carried their own machetes. I dropped them off in the backyard and they began on the ivy and the lawn, turning on water wherever they could find it. The rental people were there on a planning visit, and I got a map of where the tent and the dance floor were going to be. Hugh and Samantha stayed in the kitchen, still burning up the phone lines to Western Union, sending out invitations. Their mom stood by the sink, looking distracted.

"Mrs. Walker? Could you go for a jungle motif?"

The next four days I spent hours constructing larger-than-life plywood cutouts of climbing monkeys and bright birds to hang from trees, and representations of their snake and the iguana and that damn turkey. I wore out nine blades on my coping saw. Work with what you have! Lorenzo and Martin and I made daily afternoon runs to Armstrong's and bought every plant we could find that had orange or yellow or blue in it, and, as the sun went down, the men planted them. I found some Japanese lanterns over on Sawtelle and spent an afternoon wiring them. RSVPs began coming in. Samantha kept careful records.

I got the kids to help me as painting apprentices, showed them how to lay first and second coats of paint on my plywood, and then set them up to do some detail work after I'd painted in the big stuff, so that before their eyes plain wood began to turn into jungle mania. They loved it.

By the next Sunday morning, when the party people brought in the tent and set it up, the place looked great. I couldn't stop admiring my snake, seven feet tall with a piercing stare, turned up against the sycamore, and my green iguana, which ran to four feet and reclined in a hedge, illuminated by a couple of those battery-driven ground lamps. If parties succeeded on looks, this one was aced.

Austen and June Shaw said no to the hors d'oeuvres job, of course, but by seven Dave and Kate and some of her friends turned up, in black pants and starched white shirts. Looking good. A DJ had set up at the far end of the yard, over by the turkey. Dave checked out the newly painted pen, the stupid-looking turkey, and said to me out of the corner of his mouth, "Is this where you . . . ?"

I nodded. The music started, low and sweet. Lanterns came on. Out front, Lorenzo and Martin, spruced up, were acting as valets.

"Ah, the good life," Dave remarked, and I could only agree. What wasn't to like?

The party began. The back lawn filled up. Dave and I hopped to it, carrying out trays from the kitchen full of endive with blue cheese, and crisps dabbed with sun-dried tomatoes, and jicama with crab salad. White linen seemed to be the order of the day, and, in the middle of it all, the birthday boy came out, a fortyish guy with a puffy face. Just about as blebby as Jamey had said. Happy birthday, Michael! He stood by the snake, under flattering light, being jovial, shaking hands, taking credit for all my work.

I switched to trays of champagne and white wine. Some of the people here were my age or younger, but most were in their thirties, pushing forty. Mr. Walker sold ads for a television sports channel so most of these people were either in sports or television or advertising. Real cool or trying for it, young women in short skirts and strapless tops, basketball players looking like linen giraffes. Plain old salesmen in blue blazers, praying for Scotch. Everybody hoping this was going to be an A party, waiting for it to become one. Bob Marley came from the DJ, and a few awkward couples moved out onto the floor.

An hour later, it *looked* like an A party, as if I'd ever seen one. I noticed Dave, always the philosopher, standing at ease with an empty tray, talking earnestly to some guy. Saw Mrs. Walker, taut-faced and nuts, nudging an old fart with a purple face. Saw Hugh and Samantha, dressed up and on what passed for their best behavior, sipping what looked to be white wine out of juice glasses. People kept pouring in through the side entrance to the yard. It was dark now, and the lanterns were shining. There was about an hour more to go until dinner was served. I went back in the kitchen for another tray of wine.

And came out and did my job, just doing it, asking, "Wine? Wine? Wine?" And they all wanted it and drank it down and I took another tray of empties to the kitchen where the caterers were getting tense, and came out again, loving those lanterns, which I'd actually wired right, and my terrific plywood animals, thinking, yeah, it *is* a jungle at this place, it was cool to make it a jungle, saying, "Wine? Wine?" And the person I said it to next was Mr. Landry, who gave me a crazy look, picked up a glass, and drank all of it down.

"Wine?" I said to Angela Landry, who had been crying. Her eyes were bloodshot and swollen.

"Yes, please," she said.

Then, down in the dark, I saw another person, felt another kind of energy. I heard the kind of scream I was used to in this place, but this scream was serious. "Bob!" It came out, "Bah!"

Tod hung on to my knees for dear life.

Hugh took the tray away from me and Samantha was right there, leaning down. "Did they bring you to a grown-up party, little chiclet? What a drag that is! Come on, let's go inside. We'll play upstairs. This is so boring down here!"

Tod transferred his grip to Samantha, and she hefted him up like a sack of grain. Hugh followed along and I thought I'd better go too, through the crowded noisy kitchen, as Tod leaned over Samantha's shoulder and yelled right at me, "Bah! Bah!"

Upstairs, we pulled out Hugh's old action figures, and got Tod to laugh after a while, and then he got really giddy. He ran all around Hugh's room four or five times, touching the walls, whooping and yelling, and then he took off his shirt, holding up his arms like a champ, turning around and around, taking bows.

Samantha saw it first.

"Look at this," she said, outraged. "Just look at it."

Across Tod's thin shoulders there was a thick, red palm print. Tod looked around, stopped whirling, his point made.

"That *asshole*," Samantha said. "And I thought we were bad over here."

But the next morning when I called over there, Angela said that I must be mistaken. Then she said it was a wonderful party, and even remembered to ask if I'd done the decorations. "I think it's important for you to go on with your art," she said. "You have a lot of talent." The blue around the pool looked fabulous. And no, she didn't need anything done around the house just now because I'd done such a good job earlier in the summer.

"That's just wonderful," I said. "That's really swell."

Part Two

The job was beginning to get me down. For a week I'd been walking in mud, swimming in Redi-Crete, losing money, losing my temper. I'd spent two days with a dickhead Hollywood bachelor putting bookshelves in an apartment that already had built-in bookshelves. I bought raw wood, layered it with thinned whitewash so the grain would show, and put up the shelves. The bachelor, working out intermittently in the second bedroom—his "weights room"—decided at the end of two days that the work wasn't good enough and I wasn't going to get paid. I lost it and began yanking boards out of the wall, leaving some pretty good holes.

"Stop that!" the bachelor yelled at me. "You're defacing my property!"

"It's only your property if you pay for it," I said. "I'll sue you for fraud, you've been wasting my *time*!"

As I drove away, it occurred to me that the guy had been home for both those days and the phone hadn't rung once. He was just one more bummed-out orphan of the storm, desperate for company. But that left me with a van full of whitewashed bookshelves I didn't have any use for. I dropped off a few at Ben and Hank's, along with some cement blocks, and stowed the rest in the garage.

My next job was for a woman I couldn't seem to like, a fretful wife in her thirties who walked around her own house with a clipboard in her hand, getting organized for God knows what. She wanted all of her rooms painted white, *off* white, and we spent a morning at the paint store working on colors. I bought gallons of the stuff, custom blended, with my own money. After I'd finished the living room, she said it looked too sterile; I'd have to take the rest of the paint back and start over.

"I can't take it back. It's custom-blended." The inside of my chest felt like a brick. These women! They pretended to be dumb, they ignored the world. And thought they could get away with it. "I paid for this with my own money, remember."

I ended up taking the rest of the paint in trade, along with the brushes, stacking cans in the Micheltorena garage.

One morning I drove up Beachwood, way up in the Hollywood Hills, and parked just under the Hollywood Sign. I could feel myself getting ready to lose my temper. No lawns here, and very few homes that you could even see from the road. Just walls of trumpet vine and rockrose and ivy—not dusty and overgrown like the Walkers' but neatly clipped, and deep, watered green. The morning seemed fresh and clean and unlived-in, and made me feel out of place. Who'd need my services up here? I got out of the van and looked around.

Beachwood Drive, a slice out of a mountain, with another great view—Los Angeles by the mile. To my left, the glass towers of downtown. To my right, twenty miles away, that same pale ribbon of Pacific blue we saw from our house. No one around. The sound of a mockingbird working himself up, trying one trill after another.

I felt a sharp stab of resentment, no, make that rage. Never in my life would I be able to live like this. It wasn't just the money, although these Hollywood Hills were paved with gold. It was the ease, the confidence, the organization that I'd never be able to figure out. The best thing I could hope for in my little life would be a house in the Valley, and the last thing in the world I ever wanted in my life was a house in the Valley.

I looked at the number on my card, and the number on a redwood wall. They matched, all right. I pulled an elaborate bell-ringing thing, and a door in the wall opened.

"Bob? Come in. Did you have trouble finding the place?"

I had to adjust my attention, bend my head down. The woman talking to me stood about five feet, what my dad used to call a little-bitty thing. She looked pretty old, in her fifties somewhere, very tanned, with messy bright platinum hair, deep-set eyes. Her voice was low, husky, and she had an accent.

"Mrs. Le Clerc?"

"Come in."

She turned and walked through a narrow tiled courtyard. I ducked my head and followed her. Hanging planters of fuchsia poked at me from above and shallow pots of purple and gold pansies around my ankles made the going rough. What does she need me for? I thought. This place is *fixed* already. We got to the house and went into the kitchen. A wall of glass opened it up to that great city view.

"I was just having my coffee. Please join me."

Espresso. And orange juice straight from the squeezer. Fresh French rolls.

"What can I do for you, Mrs. Le Clerc?"

"My husband died two weeks ago. I need to go through his things. My friends have endured enough with this. And I don't want to do it alone."

"I'm sorry."

"It was a surprise, although nothing like that is ever really un-expected. He was reading, and then he wasn't. He looked up from his book and then he wasn't there anymore."

I drank some coffee. Didn't know what to say.

"That was about ten at night. I stayed in the room with him until the next morning. I pulled a chair up to his and took his hand. Even when he was still warm, he wasn't there. I'm afraid I don't be-lieve in an afterlife, and I find that I ask myself a banal question. If there's no afterlife, where did he go? Where will I go? Or you?"

"How long had you been married?"

"Twenty-four years. Not that long. We weren't young when we met."

"Can your children help?"

"We never had children. It was our choice."

"What did your husband do?"

"He was a professor of philosophy. We built this house in 1972. Buying the land took almost all we had. We put up first one room, then another. We had friends who stayed with us and worked. Shall I show you the house?"

"Please."

It was a beautiful place, peaceful and cool. It had a Mexican feel to it. There were high white stucco walls and big sheets of plate glass open to the view in each room. She had dusky Saltillo tiles across every floor, and Mexican or Central American hangings in dark corners. Japanese and Chinese low tables. There seemed to be not one library, but three of them, small and dim and clean. Down-stairs, they'd put in a big enclosed garden with dark wood furni-ture and low, vivid flowers. The colors were so clear and deep they seemed to color the air itself. I'd heard of that actually—an interior-decorating trick.

And off this garden, cut right into the slope of the hill, there was a downstairs room, their master bedroom, the walls so clean in their whiteness they seemed to have blue in them, glacier blue. A big bed, covered in sky blue. As peaceful as a church. A great place to be dead in.

"We'll be working here. I have the boxes ready. Some of my friends advise waiting to throw things away, some of them say not to wait. I don't think his shoes or shirts can save me."

All I could do was shrug. I felt like a moron. I couldn't resist glancing at my watch. Only twenty to eleven. It was so quiet in here!

"Golf shoes. He loved golf. A place he could get away from me, and from his mind. These were hiking shoes—oh, these are old. He came from Europe when he was young, just after the war. Twenty-five years later I came here from Guatemala, because of the civil unrest. My parents were German planters. I was supposed to marry into that society, but I couldn't bear the thought. And then, of course, it became impossible. We came to California in 1971 and I took a summer-school course in philosophy. Wally taught a very popular undergraduate course in Existentialism. He said that suffering was a choice we made, that we could all choose not to suffer. I thought he was mistaken, but I admired his courage. These are his teaching shoes. I think he shopped once a year, laid out his clothes every morning, put everything on without thinking."

She dropped four identical pairs of shoes into a large box, flung in tennis shoes and one pair of evening pumps, and started on another box. "He was loved by his students and hated by his colleagues. He was authentic, do you know what I mean? He'd been through the war and seen evil, and he spent his life finding weapons against it. His colleagues pursued their careers. And, of course, they disapproved of me. I was a blonde shell, a *bomb*shell. And now I have to say good-bye to his teaching suits, which he owned and used since I first met him."

"Shall I take these upstairs?"

"Not yet."

She rolled up clothes and placed them carefully in a carton.

"But later, he tended to mistake stasis for peace. He cherished quiet, lack of movement. He pared down all his motions. He was a great believer in economy."

As she bent over, I could see the back of her neck. Her hair was up. I could see tendons flex with her movements. She was so tan!

"Look at these shirts. One of our very few quarrels. He felt I should iron them. I became very haughty. A woman of good quality is not going to iron shirts like a peasant girl! But he felt that he should be cared for, physically cared for, by a person who loved him deeply. I couldn't do it. God didn't put me on earth to be a servant, I told him many times. It was one thing for us to work together on this house, quite another for me to serve him personally."

"What are your plans? Will you be staying here?" I hated the thought that this woman might end up sitting on an oval-back chair like somebody else I knew, looking out a window all alone.

"I don't know. I've spent time on this place, making it beautiful. And where would I go? When I go back to Guatemala, I have almost nothing to say to the women I grew up with. Since I have no children, in their eyes I'm worthless. They may be right, I don't know. But I do know that I've filled these boxes. Will you take them away for me? And will you come again? Can you come tomorrow, before I lose my courage, doing this?"

"Of course," I said, and began carrying up cartons, loading them in the van.

When I'd finished, I looked around for her to say good-bye and found her in the kitchen, staring out over the city. She gave me too much money, two twenties. "And these are for you, if you want them." She handed me another bundle, and I ducked my head so I wouldn't have to look at her as I said good-bye.

When I got in the van, I opened the package and found five V-necked men's cashmeres, fresh from the dry cleaners, thick and expensive. Green, coral, cream, gray, tan. A small fortune in cashmere.

So I should have felt good as I went back down the hill toward Franklin. But I didn't.

I headed for home, but stopped first on Western Avenue at the Salvation Army. I drove around the back and handed off the cartons to a man who casually slung the clothes into a huge Dumpster. All of Mrs. De Clerc's folding and rolling for nothing.

Don't you at least want to keep the suits together? I almost asked. But it wasn't my business.

"So, Mr. Le Clerc," I said, as I walked around the van, pulled myself up and climbed in. "Rest in peace, OK?"

I came by Mrs. Le Clerc's at 9:30 the next morning, and made sure not to eat breakfast before I got there. I told myself it was because of June Shaw poking around in the kitchen in spandex biking shorts chopping dates and raisins for a foul-looking granola. That was true, of course. Mornings in our house were light years away from Valerie Le Clerc's perfect espresso. But there was another aspect to it.

I'd mentioned it to Dave the night before, as we'd shot baskets down at the foot of the hill by Micheltorena Elementary.

"There's a side effect to this job." It was easier to talk if I kept messing with the ball—bounce, bounce, *shoot*, recover. "I hadn't thought of it or I'd have got into it sooner."

"Yeah?" Dave liked to say he practiced silent basketball, ball as Tai Chi. He stood in the dark playground, solid and centered, just in front of the basket, willing the ball to come to him. When it came close, he snaked out an arm, recovered, threw, scored more often than not. I ran around all over the place.

"I've been getting a lot of play. For a change. Comparatively speaking. I told you before, I think. Kind of unexpected."

Dave decided to sing. "The man comes to our house every single day, Papa comes home and the man goes away. Papa does the work and Mama gets the pay. And the man comes to *our* house every single day!" He snagged the ball, sank a basket.

"Where'd you hear that?"

"My dad used to sing it to my mom."

"If people . . . knew . . . the whole world would be out working as a handyman." I missed a shot. "I do wonder about these women, though. Don't they have anything to do? I mean, all the way around. They're sitting in houses with nothing better to do."

"That's what women do, lad. If they don't work. They sit in the house and then they buy groceries. Do men have it any better? Make stuff, sell stuff, make stuff, sell stuff. Go to war when they can't take it anymore."

He was getting off the point, as far as I was concerned. "Some of these women, they scare me."

"My dad used to say . . . If you want booty, you can't be particular." Dave snagged the ball. Mystical energy.

"If it's falling in my lap, how can I say no?"

"Yeah, but where do you draw the line?"

"June Shaw?"

We both laughed.

Parts of this conversation kept running through my mind as I pulled up in front of the Le Clerc house. I did the best I could not to notice them. I tried to focus instead on the clean smell of the damp earth in the first garden, and the smell of rosemary, and the just-watered pansies and camellias. And the smell of that great coffee. All I wanted was breakfast! I knocked on the kitchen door and she slid it open for me.

Instead of making orange juice, she'd sectioned oranges in two crystal bowls.

"What's that other great flavor in this?"

"Amaretto. To go with the almond croissants."

I ate like a king while Mrs. Le Clerc took an occasional orange section for herself and gave me a few paragraphs about her family home in Guatemala—a hacienda at the base of a beautiful mountain, where coffee plants disappeared in cloudy mists at the peak. Wide verandas, where the ladies of the house gathered in the heat of the afternoon to gossip and play canasta. The strangeness of the beginning war years when soldiers, not even out of their teens, threatened all but the very richest families. Fortunately, they were among the very richest. Long afternoons and evenings, when she and other well-brought-up girls of the area drove to the country club, sunning themselves by the pool, drinking rum-and-Cokes (with their mothers' grudging permission). They heard gunfire from time to time, but told themselves that it had to be a defective car backfiring, or maybe the *paludismo* trucks that plied the back roads squirting pesticide into stagnant ponds to exterminate malarial mosquitoes—maybe the tubes were stopped up and that's what made the popping sound. Until the smell of cordite drifted into the grounds of the club itself, and the mothers made anxious calls to the police for an escort home. Except they couldn't be sure they could trust the police.

And the final fateful morning she told me about, when she and her mother and her aunt drove fearfully to the airport, carrying only what they could take in big straw handbags, so that watching eyes in the jungle along the road wouldn't know they were leaving, but accept the flimsy idea that most likely they were driving to the airport to meet a few more visiting relations from Germany or France.

And the men in the family stayed stoically in the hacienda with the few servants and field hands whom they thought they could trust, and eventually every last one of them died in flurries of gun-fire on steaming afternoons, humid moonlit nights.

"God," I said. "That must have been awful."

Mrs. Le Clerc shot me a disapproving glance, as if to say, I give you some of my very best material, and that's all you can come up with? She cleared away the dishes. "I think today will be harder for me. We're going to sort through papers."

I'd been right the day before. There *were* three libraries in this house. She showed them off to me. Her own—Valerie's—was given over entirely to works by women. She stood me in the doorway and rattled off names—Vita Sackville-West, Anaïs Nin, Djuna Barnes. She had three paintings in here, which I frowned at, trying to get the point. A small reproduction of Our Lady of Lourdes, a nicely rendered Kwan Yin, and another smoky-looking Asian goddess with a hundred arms, an eye in the palm of each hand. It was dark in here, with a smell of dried flowers.

"When we built this house, I insisted on a place for myself. I still thought I might create something of my own."

"There's a saint, I can't remember which one, who hid bread under her cloak, and when her jealous husband ripped back the cloak the bread turned to roses."

"I'm afraid I don't follow you."

"I thought," I said lamely, "something like that might look nice in here."

The next library, no more than an alcove, held the stuff most people had. Even my mother, even my Seal Beach uncles had some of these books. Just not so many and not so organized. There was a small fireplace right in the middle of the wall, with two chairs pulled up beside it.

"My husband, when he felt sad, would come home and say, 'Can we have drinks in the snuggery?' "

"The snuggery?"

"Yes. This room."

His own study was a different story. Papers and more papers. Books mashed any old way into shelves that sagged under the weight, and more papers pushed in on top. No computer. Two filing cabinets so full that some of the drawers couldn't close.

Mrs. Le Clerc closed her eyes as though she had a headache. "I'm afraid you have to do it."

"I wouldn't know where to start."

"He retired years ago, but he never threw anything away. He liked to have a cluttered desk. To be a work in progress. He entertained his students in here until the day he died. Still working on their dissertations. Some of them going bald!"

I steered clear of the desk and headed for a file, opening the top drawer. Breathed in the smell of old paper.

Philosophy 101. Plato. Socrates. An exam in five parts. Pick three. Be specific. Cite all sources.

Jesus.

There must be a hundred copies of this one exam.

"Should I keep samples, one of each, of the things I find? These exams?"

She'd pulled a chair up to a window and sat forward with her hands in her lap, looking out, striking a posture that gave me the willies.

"There are no more students, are there? No classes *or* exams."

Philosophy 383. Sartre and Camus. Choose three of five questions. Cite all sources. Plagiarism will not be tolerated.

Another fistful of papers. I pitched them all out.

"What are these?"

"Offprints. When someone got published in the old days, the periodical would send the writer offprints of his article, and the writer would hand them out to his friends and enemies to show that his career was going well. Wally rarely published, but his colleagues did."

I began a stack of my own. I'd take them home to Dave and June and Austen, let them dig around.

Silverfish. Dust. Paper clips and staplers and erasers and ballpoints old as the hills. I got one file drawer finished.

And more of the same. Correspondence in colored cellophane folders.

"Throw them out," Valerie said. "It's over now."

He had envelopes dating back to the fifties and forties and books with pages torn, and advertisements for products that didn't even exist anymore. And of course, classroom texts, heavily underlined by the professor himself.

"Throw them out. I know what he cared for and what he hated. I don't need the books to remind me."

I was hot. The room filled with dust, and Mrs. Le Clerc didn't seem to feel like talking. I'd filled eight big Hefty bags when I heard the chime of the front door and Valerie excused herself.

In a few minutes, two young guys and a nervous woman appeared in the room with a dolly and an armload of flattened cardboard.

"Take all the books. As quickly as you can."

The woman, a pretty creature with wavy hair, said, "The university is very grateful."

I couldn't believe what I was watching. The guys hauled down books by the armload and the lady pushed out cardboard to make boxes. They loaded up a dolly, wheeled it out. The dolly came back, and left, came back, and left. Within half an hour, all the bookshelves in the room were empty.

They left. I thought I'd better speed up, and filled another seven bags. She wanted her husband gone, I'd get rid of him for her. By something like three in the afternoon, everything but the desk had been cleared out. The desk itself still had stacks all over it—those offprints, that looked pretty pitiful now, a stack of snapshots, and a collection of the weird stuff that ends up in any office—a carved box, a pewter mouse, a plastic dog with jaws that snapped, a portable shrine of the Infant of Prague. I was sweating, covered with dust, and starved. Ready to eat a horse and chase the driver.

Valerie brought in sandwiches, ham on pumpernickel with hot mustard, Perrier, and a decanter of brandy.

I sat at the office desk and wolfed down the sandwiches. I thought I knew by now why she wanted everything out. The outlines of the room were coming clear; I could see she wanted it for something else. I saw that she was watching me eat. She only had a little brandy.

"This may be the best meal I ever ate."

"You worked very hard. I'm grateful. I couldn't have done it myself. He didn't like people going through his things."

Was she afraid she'd find a secret? Another life that didn't belong to her? Something as separate from her as her afternoons at the country club were from him?

"You look tired. Should we stop for today, and you come back tomorrow? Would that be possible? Could you come around four? Do you like to paint, *house* paint? Would you like to paint this room? Not tomorrow, but later? Tomorrow, would you like to go on the roof and sweep leaves, clean out the gutters? Is four too late for you?"

I leaned up against the desk with my legs sprawled out. The brandy had gone straight to my head. All I could do was nod yes, sure I'd come back.

By the time I got down to the bottom of the hill, I'd come back to myself enough to try and get a grip. I'd forgotten to ask her for today's money, every bone in my body ached, and any thoughts of a magic afternoon seemed insanely out of the question. I thought I must have been nuts to even think of it.

In your dreams, Bob, in your dreams.

But what kind of weird dreams were they in the first place? When I thought about that, I knew I was in trouble.

I slept late the next morning and creaked when I got out of bed. I spent a lot of time in the shower, letting the water smooth out the knots in my neck. In the kitchen, I found the offprints I'd brought home scattered across the counter and floor. I went out for breakfast, did some errands, came home, felt the need for another shower, saw that the time was coming up on three.

I got in the van, stopped by a liquor store, looked for something she might like, and bought a bottle of Fernet Branca. I realized I'd cleared a grand total of about twenty bucks from two days' work—and three good meals—but I wouldn't get rich if I went on this way. (But maybe I'd learned I'd never teach for a living, or go back to a real university, ever, and maybe that was worth something.)

As I knocked on the kitchen door, I registered a scrabbling in my chest like the beginning of an acid trip, and a tightening in my groin. *You idiot,* I said to myself, and then she was there.

Old! Why couldn't I keep *that* in my mind? Why wouldn't I remember? Her tan skin had been lightly oiled, and her platinum hair was pinned loosely up off her neck again. She wore a house coat of some dark orange gauzy stuff. She smelled like spices. The whole house smelled like spices. She took the bottle from me, smiled, put it on the table. Was I fucking *nuts*?

She led me to the back garden at the bottom of the house, the one outside the master bedroom, and began asking my advice. She'd always loved trees and flowers by the house, and then a shallow patio, and then a vegetable and herb garden beyond that. But one of her friends had suggested building a deck out from the kitchen just above. That would be good for morning sun, but a deck would cast most of this downstairs area in shade, and would that be a good thing or a bad thing?

She stood under an acacia tree and sunlight dappled through it, tracing patterns on her skin and hair. There was a fig tree, and a pomegranate, and the postage-stamp flagstone patio with two chaise longues padded in deep blue canvas pushed together. Low redwood tables stood on either side with carafes of red wine and ceramic platters of figs and apricots. That spicy smell again.

"You wouldn't want to lose this." I was having trouble with my voice. "Everyone has a deck. What do you want a deck for? Nobody has this."

"I get so tired of thinking what to do. Maybe the best thing is to do nothing."

She drooped a little. Then she was lying down, the dark orange dress against dark blue. What else could I do but lie down beside her? It was so great out here, so comfortable. She poured us both some wine.

"My whole life I wanted to be an artist," I told her, and then I spaced, looking past her at green pomegranate leaves, dusty fig leaves, the blazing orange and yellow of nasturtium borders. "No one in my family had ever done anything like that before. They thought I was crazy. We're the kind of people who live in trailers. My uncles live in an old Airstream. I was an art major at UCLA. Then I worked in advertising for a few years and made a good living, and did some painting, but I still wanted to be an artist. A real one. *In my dreams*, right?"

I told her about going to Paris, about the cold and the rain and how I couldn't figure out the École des Beaux-Arts, how I didn't have the nerve. She listened, and drank, and opened up a fig, licking into it with her narrow tongue.

"I'm beginning at Otis Art Institute in the fall, you know the place? But I look at what's out there, I'm talking about *art* now, the art scene, and I can't imagine being a part of it. I don't like what they're doing. And I certainly don't know what *I'm* doing."

"I wonder if it's not life we're supposed to pay attention to. Life tells us. What we're supposed to do."

I turned to look at her. Her eyes were closed, her face tilted up a little to catch the sun as it filtered through leaves. Sun made her face glisten and I noticed that while her skin stretched taut against her jawline and cheekbones, she had those give-away tiny lines above her upper lip. The sunlight caught those lines. Coruscation, was that what they called it? Those tiny lights that the sun made on the sea?

"Your skin has coruscation from the sun. The sun keeps catching it, lighting it up."

I propped myself on an elbow and kissed her lips. Her tongue was like the rest of her, thin and dusky and aromatic. *Whoa!* What was *this*! I took off like a rodeo horse. I tried to cover her body with my own, lie down on top of her while I took off her clothes and my clothes at the same time. What the *hell* was I doing? It seemed very important to pin down her legs with my own, pin down those tan feet with my shoes, even though common sense told me I was going nowhere with this, especially with my briefs and khakis and all her orange gauzy stuff. I pulled my head back to get a look at her and she tilted her head a little to the side, her lips parted in a smile, her eyes closed. I bent my face down into the crease of her neck and breathed in as hard as I could. *Whoa!* I drew the smell into my lungs, held it, let it out. She shivered.

I got out of my clothes like a madman while she lay there, eyes closed, waiting. I began to bunch up pieces of her orange gauze and saw that she sunbathed naked. Her nipples were dark brown against her tan, flat breasts. Her body was tan, lean muscle. The hair she had down there was anchovy brown.

And that's where I went, trying to get to the source of that dusky, spicy smell. I felt her fingers tracing patterns on my neck, and thinking about it later I could say time stopped. It was a question of staying there until I found it, the source of it, *it*. I wiped my wet face with the back of my hand, and I smelled it on my hand, again.

"What is it?"

She opened her eyes, smoothed her hair, looked at me.

"What is it!"

"When you left yesterday afternoon, I soaked for two hours in a bath with Shalimar. But that was too sweet. After I'd dried, I cut lemons in half and rubbed them all over my body. I picked a sprig of rosemary and slept with it . . . *there*." She pointed a careless finger. "And a few other things this morning."

I scrambled around for a condom and came into her like a regular lover, and her lean legs wrapped around my neck. She was as limber as a chimp. I grabbed her dusty left foot and held it to my nose, inhaled lemon and spice and heavy perfume, and came.

"Whoa!" I said, "How could he have died when he had *this*?"

I felt terrible for saying it. Just terrible.

"When I saw you, I knew I had to have you. I knew it before I saw you. To keep from . . . Something that would . . ."

"Don't even tell me. I can't believe this is happening."

I came into the house quietly, after two in the morning. Austen's light was on, and I thought Dave might still be up, but I ducked right into my own room and turned on the overhead light. I held my forearm to my nose, inhaled. She was right, plain perfume would have sickened both of us, after all we'd done. But just remembering what we'd done jerked my sore dick up against my pants. It had been through the mill.

I got out of my clothes and laid out my paints in a hurry, pulled out a canvas, grabbed a #2 pencil.

Just to get the outline. A saint picture, a picture of Saint Valerie, but instead of roses, rosemary. Instead of Old Testament linen in those traditional folds, just sharp, oiled, tanned skin, with pubic hair like anchovies. A cloak of dark orange. And at her feet, glowing lemons and nasturtium. More rosemary for the halo, scratchy, dusty green all around her body. Her face, tilted to one side, expecting pleasure, happy about it. The lines above her lip, they had to be there. Tomorrow, before I mixed more paints for the hard work of it, I'd get some real rosemary, grind it in.

Ben was sick again. Hank had called Ben's new "Buddy for Life" the night before, and he'd come over and driven Ben and Hank to the emergency room, but it turned out to be the same old story. He wasn't *that* sick, and they couldn't get him in. Just the flu, they said, or an upset stomach. The Buddy—Buddy for Two Weeks, Hank called him, because that was how long he'd been assigned to them—was a nice guy, a heterosexual in his forties. He'd been in a fight with his ex-wife, who'd kept calling him on his cell phone, in the car and in the hospital waiting room. The phone kept ringing and the guy kept yelling into the phone, so after he'd driven them back home, Hank decided he couldn't come over anymore. "I told him *adiós*," Hank said. "We've got enough trouble here without going through somebody else's divorce." So then Hank called me.

It was a midafternoon in the second week in August, and hotter than hell. The heat bleached the color out of everything in sight, squeezed every drop of sweat out of every person it touched, evaporated the water and left the grease. How was it, I wondered, that the people in the paintings by old masters always looked so *bathed,* even if they'd lived in Florence in the summer? I'd answered Hank's call and come straight on over this morning, but it wasn't my idea of a good time. Not that I didn't want to help, but it was so fucking depressing.

In the five or six weeks since I'd met them, Hank had gotten a little more of their act together. He'd dealt with APLA and found that Buddy for Life. People kept wanting to walk their pets, except they didn't have any. Volunteers had brought over more linens, and plenty of rubber gloves and rubber sheets. The lady from Angel Food stopped by three times a week. Besides coming by in the afternoons, I had stayed with Ben a few evenings so that Hank could get out a little. He did go out. He was determined to "enjoy" himself. He'd had dinner at Millie's on Sunset and gone out to Dragstrip 66 on Riverside Drive. He'd been doing some body building; he'd dyed his hair a heavier black and cut it in a cooler do. But under his hip hair his face still looked like it belonged to a kid from Ohio. "I dreamed about this life for as long as I knew about it," he told me, "but I don't fit into it. No one wants me around. Except for Ben, of course."

Ben had been throwing up every twenty minutes since about six o'clock the night before. The linen situation was under control; Ben almost always had rubberized squares under his behind now like the ones they used for babies. Every time he threw up, he had some diarrhea, not much. After he was over being sick, Hank put on gloves, rinsed out the square, put it in a plastic laundry hamper. The poor kid had nothing left in his system, nothing but bile. After it came up, Hank would give him a little cup of 7-Up, which Ben drank right down, and said, "Oh, that was wonderful!" He'd lie back under a sheet and doze for exactly fifteen minutes—you could time it. Then he'd sit up on the edge of the bed, swallowing hard, and start coughing, and swallowing harder, while Hank, and now me, would start saying, "Is there anything we can get you? Do you want anything?" Until the five minutes had gone by, and the kid picked up a yellow plastic bucket and puked in it.

Then, after he was done, Ben drank more 7-Up and lifted his skinny butt so that Hank could put down a new rubberized pad. I took the bucket out back, sloshed it with a hose, left a skim of fresh water across the bottom, came back in, sat down by Hank. It was just the three of us, and the situation.

"The guy from Shanti, he calls a couple of times a day," Hank said. "He's like a stereotype. He's taken the Course in Miracles. He says he doesn't get up in the morning, not even to go to the bathroom, until he's read his lesson. And the people from Angel Food are Course in Miracles people. They tell me to expect a miracle. I can expect one as much as I want, but that doesn't mean it's coming any time soon."

It had to be over a hundred degrees in this room. I'd bought them a couple of fans from Home Depot, which moved the air around but didn't cool it off. Nothing could cool it off in here.

"I can stay a little while longer," I told Hank. "Do you want to go for another walk? Get some fresh air?"

"I could walk for fifty miles and it wouldn't change anything. You know what's weird about the Shanti people? The Angel Food people? They don't know what to do any more than we do. They're just as scared as we are." Hank closed his eyes. "I don't think I can stand this. I don't think I can go on with it."

I got up, went for a tour of the little house. There was my painting right by Ben's bed, and another painting I'd done of Hank alone where the biker poster had been. There were a few dirty dishes on the kitchen sink—I rinsed them out. I turned on a sprinkler in the front yard.

I got an idea for another painting—the Junction, just the way it was, poor and crowded, full of gang kids and immigrant families. Santa Monica pitching into Sunset, and Benjamin, sick and sweet, wonderful and splendid in every way, being assumpted into heaven. Everyone in the street looking up with polite interest.

"I've got a deck of cards in the van. Want to play some cards? Gin rummy?" I wanted to go home, but I knew I couldn't.

"Why not?"

We played through the afternoon, or at least until around seven, when Hank noticed that Ben had gone thirty-five minutes without throwing up. This was good news, he told me, and whispered that maybe they both might get to sleep through the night if Ben kept tapering off. I thought it over, thought it over some more. I couldn't get a handle on it. I couldn't figure it out. The kid was seventeen. He was going to die, going to die right here, in this time frame, in this city, in this house, probably. There was nothing I could do about it.

By 8:30 I couldn't stand it over there a minute longer. I couldn't think of a good reason to leave so I just left. Hank stood at the front door and watched me go. I could feel him looking at me, but I didn't look back.

Driving home, I began to freak all over again. I hadn't worn gloves all the time I'd been handling Ben's vomit. I knew I didn't have any cuts on my hand, but there was the beginning of a canker sore somewhere inside my mouth. (I remembered one of my granddad's raddled old girlfriends coming up to me once at a picnic: "Did you ever have a sore right *here*?" And then having to listen to some terrible story about venereal disease back in World War II.) Suppose I'd stuck my fingers in my mouth this afternoon? Bitten my fingernails? It could happen.

"Suppose you're fucking nuts," I said out loud. "That could happen too."

Still, I felt queasy as I pulled into the garage. My stomach heaved. "Probably just a virus. The kid probably just had a virus, and maybe I caught it," I muttered. Then I thought, damn *right* he has a virus, and maybe I caught it! But as I stepped down from the van, something else caught my attention: big, loud man's sobs. Coming from the kitchen.

Austen had installed himself in his favorite place, the empty refrigerator alcove. He sat on his broad butt with his knees up to his shoulders and sobbed into the hem of his sweatshirt. The whole front of his shirt was soaked with tears and snot. June Shaw knelt down by him trying to pat his shoulder. Instead of being grateful for the attention, he tossed his head away from her and kept on roaring. Even Dave had come out to the kitchen to see what was up with the guy.

"What happened?" I asked. I had to raise my voice above the noise.

"He got some kind of letter," Dave said, "from the university. He's out."

"I'm not well," Austen sobbed. "Call a doctor. I'm dying. I'm going to die."

"Well, *shit*," I said. I went to the fridge, found a beer on my shelf, opened it up. "What a fucking crock."

That caught June's attention. "Toad!" she said. "Scum!" She scrambled to her feet and shoved me hard in the chest. "Oaf!"

I clenched my fist and raised it, remembered she was a woman, and stopped.

"He got dropped from graduate school! That's the end of his career! It wouldn't matter to someone like you. You couldn't understand it!"

"What are you picking on me for? I didn't do anything. How'd he get kicked out?"

By this time Austen had managed to curl his big sleepy body into a fetal ball. He mashed his face against the far wall of the alcove and turned his back to us. The partition shuddered with his sobs. He made a hell of a racket.

"He missed the German deadline because of his work on the hunger strike. We'll have them up on charges for this!"

"But didn't he miss his deadline? Isn't that what the letter said? So, he knew what he was doing, didn't he?"

"Moron!" June really did seem upset.

"I just want to ask both of you something." And only my day with Hank and Ben would have allowed me to ask it. "The whole world knows there aren't any jobs out there for what you people are trying to do. So what are the both of you even doing in school? Why don't you get real jobs, so you don't have to pull this stupid shit any more?"

She shoved me again, hard. For a second time! This time I shoved her back. She went flying across the linoleum, landing with a thud against the stove.

"OK, *buster,*" she shouted at me, "get ready for the lawsuit of your life!"

But I felt something in my body, beginning somewhere in my solar plexus and flooding up behind my ears. I watched myself, about one-tenth of me still calm and interested while the other nine-tenths began to go berserk.

"Give it a rest, you . . . baboon! Get out of this room before I break your scrawny arms. Out. Out!" I surprised myself. It wasn't like me.

She worked her lipsticky mouth but she didn't move. Maybe she couldn't.

"You aren't worth my time," I told her. "You!" I said to the beige lump in the alcove. "Get up, you worthless heap!" I watched as my own running shoe shot out and began prodding Austen's soft back. "Get up. Get up! Be a man. *Fake* it, for Christ's sake!"

"I'm not well," Austen said. "I've been through a lot. People have died in my family."

I kept pushing at him. "Do you know anything about it? You don't know anything about anything."

"Don't take that from him!" June Shaw screamed, but I showed her my clenched fist again, and she took a step back.

"Get up! Act like a man."

"Maybe he'd like to go to his room," Dave suggested, but I grabbed the back of Austen's shirt and tugged. "You think life is awful? *I'll* show you awful."

"Don't! You'll tear my clothes." But one way or another, Austen got up.

"Wipe the crap off your face. I'm taking you for a ride."

Austen sat beside me in the van while we made the short run down to Manzanita. His big body still quivered and sighed every once in a while, but you could see he was getting curious too. We parked and I went around to the passenger side to open the door. "Get out, asshole. We're paying a visit."

Hank opened the door right away. "How'd you know? He's gotten worse again."

I could feel my temper draining away. "I've got a friend here, Alec Austen. He wants to help out. He's going to sit with you for a while. I'm going out for some burgers for all of us. And some more beer."

Hank spoke right to Austen, telling his same old story. It didn't seem to matter that he was talking to a stranger. "I can't do it anymore. I know I have to, but I'm afraid I can't. I'm afraid of what I'll do."

Austen let himself be led into the next room. I watched his face change as he saw Ben.

"Back in a while," I told them. They didn't answer.

Through the evening, Austen helped with the bucket and rubberized pads. In between, the three of us sat out in the living room, talking, keeping our voices down.

"Where's his medication?" Austen asked at one point. "Even a Thorozine suppository for the nausea would have to help. And all the other drugs. Why doesn't he have them? Aren't there clubs where you can buy them wholesale?"

Hank explained again that they'd just come out from Ohio, that they didn't have much money. That they couldn't go to their families. That some organizations were helping, but they couldn't afford protease inhibitors. Or much of anything. I watched that familiar expression of sullen outrage come over Austen's face.

It was so late by now, and I was so tired. I sat nodding in my chair, getting up with the other two every twenty minutes, until, about one, the intervals began stretching out again. The kid appeared to settle down. It looked like he might be tuning up for a real sleep.

"I guess we'd better be going," I said.

"I'm staying here," Austen whispered to Hank. "Is that all right?"

I drove home, aching for sleep.

So, by the end of August, Austen had another cause. He lurked in the hall outside his bedroom when he was home, and all of us took to using the back door to avoid his little sermons. "Did you know that thalidomide can stop mouth ulcers from AIDS in only four days? Not only that, but it significantly reduces the amount of the virus, the viral *load,* in everyone who takes it? People have to organize to outsmart the drug companies. All *they* want to do is get rich off this epidemic. Why would you want to eliminate your own best market? Does Philip Morris try to get people to stop smoking?"

Austen gave us all reproachful stares, as though we'd been out spreading AIDS. But June Shaw practiced militant abstinence, and Dave's Tai Chi method hadn't worked with sex, so far.

"You're the Typhoid Mary, Bob," Dave told me, trying to joke about it. "You're the one who turned him on to this. And you're the king of unsafe sex around here."

I had more than one shiver of doom thinking about just that. I always had plenty of condoms but never quite enough. I even thought, sometimes, of going down to be tested. But I didn't go. Common sense told me I was OK, but late at night, lying awake, common sense didn't always work. And there was Austen the hall sentry now, telling everyone who came through the front door to repent, abstain, refrain.

So, none of us came through the front door if we could help it.

It was late, late August, the worst time of the year in LA. Dog days. August 18th was my absolute last chance to enroll in Otis for the fall semester, their last semester in their "picturesque" downtown location. I had to get my portfolio downtown quick if I wanted either a scholarship or financial aid. I loaded up some stuff and rolled on down in my van to Wilshire Boulevard by MacArthur Park. The admissions people liked my work, although I'd never managed to do the self-portrait. I got in, with a partial scholarship and a substantial student loan. Instead of illustration or surface design—which would at least guarantee me a future career with some commercial outfit—I chose a couple of classes in fine art, kind of a last wave at what I knew now I could never be. Classes were due to start September 3rd.

The end of summer. I came home from a day replacing doorknobs and water faucets in a bad motel on Western Avenue, stinking of sweat and roach powder. I couldn't get over the idea that some people deliberately chose to live in ugliness, as if there weren't enough of it around already. I'd seen unflushed toilets, even with water in the pipes, because people were too—what? depressed? demoralized? trashy?—to move their arms up to a flushing position. I'd seen bathtubs filled with magazines, because people hadn't planned on taking a bath any time soon. And roaches. My God.

I ducked into the shower and heard screams from the kitchen, female screams, almost as bad as Mrs. Walker's when the snake got out. I knew I should go over and see the Walkers, she'd called and left a couple of messages, but I couldn't. They wanted too much from me, these women. They thought I was there to fix stuff for them and have sex. I was function and form to them, not content. "They don't care about the *real* Bob," I said out loud as I showered. I meant it to be a joke on myself, but my voice came out serious and bitter. The screams were still going on as I got dried.

In the kitchen, June Shaw held the telephone to her head and shrieked into it. She wore a white lace bra and panties, a cardigan sweater and tennis shoes.

"I've always paid back every loan I've got from you *with interest!* Ten percent interest! I will *not* type my life away like you did. I *will* have a career, whether you help me or *not!*"

I slid past her to the dining room, where Dave had opened his shoe box and was rolling a joint. He had a ball of hash about the size of a thumb in front of him, with a nice pile of shavings. Dave sprinkled them in with the mounded weed, then licked and twisted the paper.

"Want some?"

"Yeah." I reached in my wallet and pulled out some twenties.

"Not necessary."

"Take it. For next time."

Dave folded the money into his pocket. "Hot as hell."

"*Tell* me. I must have had five thousand cockroaches on me today."

"Hard day at the office, dear?"

"Ah, man . . ." I sat down and shook my head. I felt like shit.

Dave gestured toward the kitchen with his head. "She's having a guy over for dinner tonight. Wants to put food on this table. Wants me to move my stuff."

Of all the women in the world, we had to be living with this one.

"OK," I said. "Let's do it now. It'll only be worse later." The hash gave me that itchy feeling in my chest, and I took another deep drag on the joint. I heaved myself up and grabbed a pile of books. Dave took another one, and we stowed them under the sideboard. Two more moves and the table was clear, except for the shoe box and the hash, which we took with us to the sunken living room.

"She's not going to like this," Dave said. "She was looking forward to another fight."

"Her mother's getting it now."

"Yeah. Would you say it was *hot* around here?"

I went back down the hall to my room to take off my shirt and hang it up. The door to Austen's room was open. "Did you know there's a church in Pasadena that does more proportionately for AIDS victims in this city than Shanti and APLA put together?"

"No," I said. "How's Ben? I'm not going over this afternoon."

"The same."

Dave waited for me out on the living room couch, and we spent the next couple of hours getting seriously stoned.

June's date stood her up. By that time it seemed like too much trouble to move everything back in the dining room. By eight o'clock the sun had gone down, and by nine it got dark. One more day gone.

No one bothered to turn on the lights. Dave and I sprawled on the couch. June and Austen were in here some place.

"I have to decide what I want to do after I graduate," June said. Her voice was surprisingly low. "I want to do women's studies, but there's no point to it. Men hate women. I have to be well known in my field, whatever field it is, and the deck is too stacked against women."

"At least you're still in school." But Austen didn't sound too messed up about it.

"I want a life. A life. Just a life." Dave talking.

"You have a life," I said. It seemed like it took an hour to say it.

"I don't think so. I don't think we do. Do you know where we are? Halfway up a hill. People don't even know where we are. We're like the clear skin between zits. They can't even see us. They can't even find us. They don't know we're here."

"You have to do stuff. *Deeds*," Austen said. "You have to have a reason."

"My mother hates me." June reached out in the dark, took a joint from my fingers.

"Christ's sake, June. She doesn't *hate* you. Isn't that kind of *old*? That whole idea?"

"She does, though. Never liked me at all."

Dave coughed. "None of us are married. We don't have children. None of our parents have ever even seen this house. In the simplest philosophical terms, we aren't here."

"We're here." Austen's sweaty face was round as a pie plate. It moved as he spoke. "We're here. But there's so much to do. I can see that. I'm afraid we can't do it."

Moonlight shone through the picture window. My eyes saw them all in outline: Dave, on my right, slumped on the couch in perfect relaxation, and then the square of moonlit glass and the piano that nobody played, and then Austen, crouched on a thrift-shop hassock, tormenting himself as usual, poor guy. Down on the floor, all white skin and right angles, was the electric June. Where were our families? Our parents, our children? We're all we've got right now, I thought. This is what we've got. The room, which never seemed too grounded to begin with, slipped its moorings and sailed with us across the sky. You can't worry too much about a speck of cosmic dust, I thought, sailing away. It isn't worth the effort.

"The thing is to be famous. Make them *know* we're here." June's voice had an interesting tremor to it tonight, like a scratchy violin. Probably from yelling so hard.

"Your voice," I said, "sounds like a violin."

"Man," Dave said. "These artists."

"I'll never be. An artist. You know what I need? A cold beer for my hashed-out throat."

I woke up the next morning, and knew before I opened my eyes that I wasn't alone. Information came in; a head resting by my head. A bed that wasn't mine. When I did open my eyes, there was the sun and that damn eucalyptus. Not my tree, though. This was the corner room. Kate's room. June's room.

I moved, very slightly. Her arm came further over across my ribs. I wasn't going to be able to sneak out of this.

Quietly, I moved my head back to see her more clearly. As long as I'd done this fool thing I might as well pay attention.

Her skin was perfectly pale and very clear. How would you paint it, that skin? Her lips without the lipstick had a nice old-rose tint. I could see her hand on my chest. She had long fingers, close-clipped nails. She was very clean. Thin arms. She breathed quietly. She smelled good.

She opened her eyes and blushed.

I kept quiet, waiting for the cyclone.

She got up, carefully keeping her back to me, went to the closet, put on a robe, and went out to the bathroom. I could have jumped up then, sprinted down the hall. I could pretend it never happened. I stared at her few outfits in the open closet. That shiny brown suit. Those matching brown oxfords.

She came back in quietly, closed the closet door and the door to the hall. She'd combed her hair and splashed water on her face.

She sat down on the bed, looked at me, glanced away.

"Listen," she said.

I listened.

"I'm sorry." Her voice still had that scratchy violin texture. It made me take hold of her hand.

"No. Don't. We can't do this again."

I widened my eyes. *Why,* I telegraphed. *What on earth do you mean?* I didn't dare open my mouth.

"There's a disparity, an intellectual disparity. It's not your fault."

I turned my head away from her.

"There's no room for a person like you in my life. We have to go on living as though this never happened."

Acting completely on their own, my hands opened her robe. Her breasts stared watchfully out into the distance. Her body had a separate personality. A nice one.

"*Don't!* We have to pretend we were never together."

I let the robe fall back in place. Remembered the bed had another whole side to it and rolled on out. I found my shorts and got them on some way. I pulled on my T-shirt. Then I stopped for a minute. Put a hand on her cheek. She blushed again, hung her head.

I got out of there quick. Headed for the kitchen. Poured some coffee.

Dave was already up, and looked at me with something like awe. "God's gift to women," he suggested. "Would that be it?"

All I could do was shake my head. Words failed me.

A few days after my night with June Shaw, I stood in the driveway of the house while a nice woman in her thirties wrapped me up in crepe-paper ribbons. I wore a shirt and shorts and tennis shoes, which left my arms and legs free to be wrapped. The woman had lettered a sign that she fastened around my neck:

ONE FULL DAY OF SERVICE

ONCE A WEEK FOR

SIX GLORIOUS WEEKS

She fooled around with extra crepe-paper strips, tying a big floppy bow around my neck.

June came out the door, dressed today in barf-green socks, green shorts and shirt, and a Donald Duck baseball hat pushed back on her head. She took in the two of us and sneered. "Somebody's present? Aren't you *farfetched!*"

"Yeah?" I said. "Look who's talking!"

"Who is that person?" my wrapper asked.

"She lives here."

"A roommate?"

"Up to a point."

"Well, you *will* be a present. A nice gift. Remember, we want you to go the full eight hours, ten to six, or maybe eleven to seven. It's the time as much as the work. We all chipped in for this. Shelley might want to send you home but you just stay, keep her company. We're all so worried about her. She doesn't know what hit her. Once a week for six weeks. See if you can cheer her up."

"I may have to speed up the process. I'm going back to school in a week or so. What happened again? She broke up with her husband?"

"He did that thing where he didn't come home from work one night. He only talks to her now through a lawyer. She had no idea it was coming."

"How do you know her? Did you go to school together?"

"The park. We all take our kids there. We've known her from her first one. That's three years ago. She doesn't show up anymore."

I was wrapped up like a mummy by now. The only thing left was to hoist myself into the van. The woman getting me as a gift lived right here on the hill, only two blocks away. I wished that I could get a look at myself dressed as a present, but that wasn't going to happen. I took a check for today's work in advance, grabbed a helium balloon she handed me, zipped along Dahlia and turned right on Micheltorena toward Sunset, heading down for less than a block.

Again, the unmowed lawn tipped me off. That, and a few dozen shitty plastic toys on the porch. The house looked like it might be ready to burst into tears. I got out, walked up the path, and knocked on the door.

The woman who answered was taller than I was but looked at least ten years younger. She looked like a great big child.

"Shelley?"

"What is it?"

"I'm a gift."

"I don't want one." Her face was swollen and pink.

"Your friends—all of them from the park—got together to give me to you as a gift. What does it say?" I fumbled with my sign, turning it so I could read it. " 'One full day of service once a week for six glorious weeks.' I'm a handyman. So put me to work."

It was a crappy little house, and it was a fucking mess, just for a change. The windows were closed and the summer air had cooked up that familiar smell of rotten food and very old diapers. Christ, I thought. I'm a handyman, not a housemaid. I watched my step as I followed her out to the kitchen table, where she must have been sitting. I passed a kid sleeping on the couch, one crying over in the corner, and, here on the table, a third one, sweaty and white and half asleep, strapped into a baby seat.

"What do you want to do?" She didn't seem the least bit surprised or pleased.

"Could you give me a hand getting unwrapped?"

She only looked at me as I started pulling off my strips of crepe paper.

"Should we start with some laundry? Do you have a machine here?"

She nodded. She seemed unconscious, totally dazed. I looked around the kitchen. It was something like the Walker house the first time I'd seen it, every inch of surface covered with dirty dishes and dirty clothes and kids' crap of every kind, but this place was small and cramped and old and dark. I found a machine on the back porch, checked to be sure there was detergent, and put in the first load, bending down and picking up stuff right next to my feet, right where I stood. *Pòco a pòco.* Another world going down the drain. How many people around the city were in a fix like this? How long had she been like this?

"Do you mind if I open a couple of windows?" The smell of the place was close to making me gag. I went back into the kitchen— there wasn't any dishwasher—ran water in the sink, and began washing dishes. She sat at the table, not even looking at me, and two of the kids still went on crying. How could things get so bad? How could anybody let things get like this?

I filled the drainer with a first batch of clean dishes, went to the back door, opened it, and checked out the yard: just a sad trash heap of weeds and broken toys. But the fresh air was good, and that gave me an idea. I found an empty trash can, put it on the porch, and made a run through the house picking up bags of used Pampers off the floor, throwing them in the trash. Then I opened up all the windows, every window in the damn house.

Two hours later I was still at it. Loads of laundry, batches of dishes. I hit the bedrooms and peeled off dirty sheets. One kid who'd been crying quieted down and napped on the floor. The woman—Shelley—had some papers, along with the baby, on the kitchen table. She stared at them and ignored me. Around one in the afternoon, I said, "Would you like me to go out and get us some hamburgers?"

She barely nodded her head. I got a little irritated. I'd been working my ass off! Still, I got in the van, peeled out, hit a McDonald's and the mom-and-pop down at the Junction, came back with three burgers, six cartons of milk, some bread and peanut butter. And a huge box of Pampers.

Back at the house with Shelley and the baby, I pulled some more curtains back, cleared a patch among the papers, and noticed that they were bills. And that she was crying again. God! These leaky women!

"Have some lunch and you'll feel better." I handed her a burger and went out to the kitchen for some clean glasses. She chewed down the burger and drank all her milk. The whole time, tears dribbled down her cheeks.

"What are you doing there?" I said, conversationally. I certainly wasn't going to ask her how she'd gotten into a situation like this.

But it was the wrong question. She began to cry out loud.

"I can't do it. I don't know how."

She was covering a checkbook with her hand. I could see the number, 101. A new account.

"They say they'll cut off the phone if I don't pay the bill."

"Did your husband leave you without any money? Is that it?"

"No. I get two thousand a month until the divorce. And he's paid that twice, direct to the bank. But I've never written a check. He said I'd never be able to figure this out, and I can't."

"What do you mean, you can't?" And I thought that June Shaw would have taken this woman out and shot her for gross incompetence.

Like a bad kid, she moved her hand away from the checkbook a half-inch at a time. "I can't figure it out," she whispered. "He said I couldn't do anything and I can't. I don't know how to do it." Next to where it said PAY TO THE ORDER OF, she had written *two hundred and two dollars.*

"I've never written a check in my life. I married Sydney the day I got out of high school and he said he'd take care of everything. He did! He took care of things. But why did he *do* it? Why did he even marry me if he was going to do this? How could he be so mean?"

"Wait, wait. We can fix this." I found some paper towels to clean up the remains of the burgers, checked to see that the rug rats were still dozing, gathered the bills up into one stack. There weren't that many. I opened the checkbook, told her to mark 101 *void* and said, "It's easy. And don't worry if we make a mistake. We can fix it." An hour later, the paid bills were in a stack.

"Stamps?"

Her lips started quivering again and I said, "No! Stop! I can't take the waterworks!"

"Waterworks?"

"No more *crying*! Please. Now, I need your help sorting some of the clean clothes. Do you remember which stuff belongs to which kid?"

She did, sort of.

And another two hours saw the last of the dishes done, the beds aired and changed. The kids were all awake by now, looking dazed, like they'd been through a bomb blast. Shelley, raw-boned and fully miserable, had gone back to the table, watching me work.

"This won't do any good," she told me. "You have to know that. You can fix this up all you like, but it doesn't change anything. I figured that out. You clean something up, it just gets dirty."

"Where's your family? Where's your mom and dad?"

"They said I was big and stupid and I thought, all right, you want me to be nothing, I'll *be* nothing. But I *can* do this, I can get married and you'll never see me again. And so I did. I'll never ask them for anything."

"You don't see them?"

"No, because then they'd see they were right, that I'm stupider than they even thought, so, *no*."

"They don't know your husband left?"

"They don't even know where I live. And that's it. That's all I'm going to say about it."

"OK," I said. "Here's what we're going to do next. We're putting these kids in the tub, all of them, and soaking some of the dirt off. What are their names?"

"Jennifer, Sophie, and Spencer. They're three, two and almost one. And don't ask me why so many. I don't *know* why so many!"

I put them in the tub with a squirt of detergent, sat Shelley down on the toilet to watch them, put in one last load of filthy wash, then came back.

"Did he leave you a car?"

More crying. God, she was tiresome.

"He left a car, but I don't drive. He said I was too dumb to drive."

"Do you have any plans about what you're going to do?"

"No. *No.* Kill myself, probably."

I'd found some clean shirts and shorts and pulled the kids out of the tub one by one. Dried them off, dressed them.

"Here's the deal, Shelley. You're going to take a shower. I'll watch the kids while you do it. Be sure to wash your hair. You'll feel better."

Out in the living room, I tried talking to the little rats, who were about as outgoing as their mom. But when she came out, drying her hair on a towel, at least she looked a little better.

"I'm going to go out and do some shopping for you," I said. "If you sit out on the porch, you'd get some fresh air, you'd feel better. The kids, too."

I jammed the van down to a Von's and stocked up on more milk, Pampers, baby food, canned soup, cereal, hot dogs, orange juice, vitamin pills, ice cream, cookies. When I came back, they were still lined up on the porch steps.

It was close to seven by now, but I didn't feel like I could go home. It was as though they'd melt, completely unravel, if I turned my back on them.

"So, Shelley? I know you have these good girlfriends, because they gave me to you as a present. Can you call one of them?"

"I really don't know them all that well."

"OK. OK. This is what we're going to do. We're going to open up some soup. We're going to have some dinner. Then I'm going to clean up. Then I want you to watch television until ten tonight and then try to get some sleep. I'm not supposed to come by until next week, but I'll be by tomorrow. Try not to let the stuff pile up. Put the dirty clothes in the washer right away. Rinse the dishes right away." I looked around the grim little living room. "What's your favorite color?"

"Yellow. And blue, I guess."

"You like flowers?"

"Sure."

"I'll bring you a present tomorrow. Try to keep everything a little bit picked up. I know it doesn't mean anything in the long run, but give it a shot."

Before I got to bed at one in the morning, I'd turned out one very nifty canvas of yellow daisies and one of bright blue lobelia. Between the grocery money and the art supplies, my day put me in the red about ten bucks. Well, fuck it!

The next day I was over there by seven, running an old manual lawn mower through the dead grass of the front lawn. After I whacked a couple of nails in the living-room walls and stuck up the pictures, I looked over at the big horsey girl and saw the beginnings of a chapped-lip smile.

"Looks good," I said. "Now. I'm supposed to be back in six days, but I'll probably stop by in a day or two. I want you to have some lists made up for me. What needs to be done around here, and what you'll be needing to buy, and . . . what you think you might be doing with your life. Don't even think about arguing with me, Shell! I'm going to be over here, and I'm going to be needing those lists."

I checked the kids; they looked OK. I looked at the drab house, the bright pictures. "OK, Shell? Are you listening to me?"

I drove the couple of blocks back home. It was no more than

10:30 in the morning. Just twenty-four hours since I'd been wrapped up like a present.

I stumbled into the house, called one of the women who'd hired me, and told her they'd have to take turns checking up on Mrs. Ross. I left a note for Dave asking him how he felt about doing some house painting. Then I hit the bed and tried to get some sleep, but I couldn't. The world was too damn sad.

The third morning I drove over to Shelley's house with a long narrow painting of an iguana for Baby Spencer. I liked how it looked; green and gold with Thal-Green scales on its belly and bright red claws that looked like polished nails. I brought two more flower paintings for Jennifer and Sophie's room, sweet peas, pink and blue. Very girly, but what the hell, they were girls. I hung around there for a couple of hours and talked to Shell.

That night I brought Dave by and we both rolled around on the floor for a while, playing with the kids. It was great but weird to see how just that little bit of attention could change them. And dropping by kept Shelley from sliding back into her coma.

She'd been good about her lists. I'd brought her different colored pens. In green ink, she wrote down groceries, in blue, what the kids might need, in purple, what the house needed.

The fourth day she was ready for me—beds made, kitchen cleaned up, the kids in pretty good shape and ready to go. We were going to pick up some clothes at Target. I'd already gotten her to throw out any stuff that was too grungy, or that wouldn't fit anybody anymore.

I'd been pestering the toddlers and their mom about their favorite colors and what they wanted to do. I was beginning to get the idea that maybe you couldn't change the world but you could paint sadness over, brighten the whole thing up. And maybe the bright stuff would bleed down into the interior and start changing it. It couldn't hurt! And here Shelley was, the big horsey girl, on the fourth day, her hair washed, in a clean sundress, pale but determined, ready to start.

"I couldn't do any of this if you weren't here," she told me, as we piled into the van and she buckled Spencer into his car seat.

"You used to before."

"Not really. Syd works in the clothing business downtown and he never let us go out by ourselves. He'd bring stuff home, all the stuff he couldn't sell, or what his friends couldn't sell. That's why we all look so lame. Then he'd tell us we *looked* lame and he didn't want to be seen with us! So he didn't take us with him to very many places. This is harder than writing checks, almost. I don't . . . I haven't been in . . . like even a mall, since high school. I don't know what sizes the kids are. I don't know, oh, where to buy a bedspread."

Christ! I wanted to say. Why'd you stay with that crazy creep! Why'd you hook up with him in the first place? But I'd said something like that yesterday and she'd almost defended him, saying that she was the one who got pregnant and she was opposed to abortion and she was the one who, after the first two girls, had thought that maybe a son might put Sydney in a good mood. She was the one who let the house go, and herself, so that Sydney could hardly bring himself to look at her. "I think," she'd said, "he didn't know what he was getting into any more than I did. He thought he was getting just a teenaged girl, and I was. But that's a stupid person to marry."

Sydney had even hit her a few times, but she defended him. "I would have hit *myself*, if I could have figured out how to do it." I could see her point, but I'd reminded her that Sydney-the-Creep had kept her away from her old friends, and wouldn't take her out, and just plain treated her so mean for so long that finally she ended up agreeing with that creep on his creepy assessment of her.

"Yes, but he—"

"We're not going to talk about The Creep anymore! We're going to talk about you and the kids. If you had seven pieces of clothing for each one of you, which ones would they be, and what color would they be? Make a list of them, right now."

She had. The lists were ready right now.

She sat in the passenger seat beside me, breathing deeply as I headed down Micheltorena and took a right on Sunset. Baby Spencer had already fallen asleep and the two girls, dressed up and on their best behavior, looked out the windows in the back. This was a big deal for them. Man! This job was a heartbreaker. The best thing was not to think about it. Not to give it a thought.

Target shared a parking lot with a Stroud's and a few other places. We took our time in Target, finding a nice girl to help us. I told the clerk that the kids had grown so fast nobody knew what size anybody was anymore. The girl helped them and our big shopping cart filled up with shorts and bright-colored tennis shoes and underwear.

Then I said to Shelley, with a sappy grin, "Now, *honey*, we've got to find something for you!"

She looked like she might tear up again, so I nudged her and said, "Color! Remember your favorite color. And let's go find some stuff."

We bought her three big T-shirts in white and yellow and navy blue, with shorts to match. And tennis socks with gold lace on the cuffs, and white tennies.

It was still early, no more than eleven. Out in the killer sun, I noticed a Fantastic Sam's and herded them all in for haircuts. The guy, a sweating Middle Easterner, made all kinds of faces at their raggedy-ass cuts but shampooed and clipped and snipped, and in less than an hour they all looked pretty good.

Then I grabbed Shelley's house list, checked out the kids, who seemed in a daze of happiness, figured they were up for one more errand, stashed what we'd already bought in the van, and rolled everybody into Stroud's.

"Two bedspreads, three pillows, something for the crib, and we'll get the rest later. Pick your favorite color now!"

The girls had no trouble picking lavender cotton for their twin beds and Shelley went straight to a swirling floral print that had a lot of light gold in it. "Because when I said yellow, I really meant gold." With no hesitation at all, she bundled pillows into their basket, and when we got to the cash register she had her checkbook ready, with her Social Security card as identification.

"Don't you have a driver's license?"

"I don't drive," she reminded me. Incredibly, Shelley started laughing, and looked over her shoulder at me.

"Before this month is over, Shell, you will."

I had a bright idea in my mind. I bought them all more burgers at McDonald's, then headed south on Vermont to LA City College, paid to park, and hustled them all out onto the lawn in front of the Administration Building for a picnic. "Because I just wanted you to see how close this place is to your house, Shell, and how easy it would be to take some courses."

She looked trembly. "The one thing Sydney promised is that I'd never have to work. He said if I stayed home with the kids, I'd never have to work. So I don't have to go to school, do I?"

"Staying home all day with three kids is a regular barrel of laughs. I couldn't help noticing how much you've been enjoying it."

Sitting on the grass with the sun shining down on her freshly cut hair, she looked absolutely young. Of course, she wasn't much older than any of the students out here with us on the lawn.

"I know I have to earn a living some day."

"Nah. That's not what I'm talking about. I don't want you to learn how to mess with somebody else's medical records or work on the computer for some asshole. Remember, Shell, what I've been saying to you? *What's your favorite color?*"

"I don't know. I don't."

"That's why you take college classes—to find out what you like."

"I'm too stupid."

I didn't even try and argue with her. "What's your favorite subject? There has to be something."

She looked at me, drawing a blank. The kids, who might have been carriers for sleeping sickness, had crashed by now, all three of them, their cheeks against the grass.

"You don't want them to grow up hearing you say that, that you're stupid?"

"No!"

"Well, so? I'm going into the Ad Building to pick up a fall catalog and schedule of classes. When I come back, I want you to have a list for me. OK? OK?"

When I came back, she did. French. History. Music.

It was a start.

By the time we got home it was after three in the afternoon. Shelley and I worked together putting things away, and put on the bedspreads. She actually laughed a couple of times. I couldn't help it, I was impressed. The hellhole with four suffering souls in it I'd come into just a few days ago had changed into a plain, semi-cheerful cottage with a nice mom and three cute kids. They still seemed sandblasted by life, but they weren't going to kill themselves anytime soon.

"You know," I said, as we drank lemonade and rested, "I have two thoughts. Dave's going to help me for a few days doing some painting in here, OK? And—what about a class in estate planning?"

"What's that?" At least she didn't look like a whipped dog, admitting there was yet another thing she didn't know.

"You know those ads on television, where they say if you'd started saving a hundred a month when you were twenty-one you'd have a billion bucks to retire on when you're sixty-five? Well, you're only twenty-two. And you can certainly spare a hundred a month, maybe more. You just have to learn how to invest."

"I can't do that!"

"Neither can I. But if you took a class in it you could teach me. You could give me tips."

"That would chap his ass!"

"Excuse me?"

"It would chap Sydney's ass if I got rich!"

"Then I think you've got to do it."

"I can't go to school. It's a nice dream, but I can't drive and there's nobody to stay with the kids."

"That's your car in the driveway?"

"Sydney's other car."

I jumped up, grabbed the phone, dialed my own number. "Dave? I'm at Shelley's. Can you come over for an hour and watch her kids? I'm going to give her a driving lesson."

In five minutes Dave was there. I had to tease her and threaten her but pretty soon I maneuvered Shelley out to the car, where she sat in the driver's seat, telling me she couldn't do it. But then she changed her mind. Jerking Sydney's Acura into reverse, she made a wide, crazy circle out into the street, crunched into first, and careened down onto Sunset. I sat in the passenger seat and prayed. But she did remarkably well, so well that I got her to stop by a nursery to pick up a couple of pony packs of marigolds. "Since I didn't know until today gold was one of your *real* favorite colors."

Her smile was unexpected, and still incredibly new. She smiled as she drove us back, remembered to signal on Sunset when she turned left, and she didn't spook going up the hill. She even hit the driveway pretty well, before she stopped the car with a tremendous jolt. Dave and the kids waited on the porch and waved. I was proud of her, blown away by this whole Pygmalion trip.

"I did take Driver's Ed, you know," she said. "I got a B in it."

She looked new and fresh. I took the credit, wished there was someone I could tell about it.

That same week, I showed up at Valerie Le Clerc's dressed to drive her on what she said were "important errands," in pressed khakis, blue shirt, nice tie, white linen sports jacket. I got a kick out of her asking me for this. I'd taken the van to be washed and stowed my handyman junk in the hall outside my room, which made June Shaw sick. "What a dilettante!" she'd said, as she surveyed my hammer, screwdrivers, miter box, boom box, and then, checking out my dressed-up self, "Going to the *doctor?*" which she evidently thought of as the last word in cutting insults.

I hopped up into my clean-and-neat vehicle, headed on out. It was one in the afternoon, a scorcher of a day, but Valerie seemed fresh as dew waiting for me in a pale gray pantsuit with a long lavender scarf. She wore wraparound aviator glasses and looked too cool for words. I liked her a lot.

"Where to, Madame?"

But, man, she wasn't young. Her neck showed it. The backs of her hands showed it. Cruising down Beachwood, I argued with myself. Who *cares*? Who's the person in charge who tells us who we should want and who we shouldn't? I consciously thought *rosemary* to stop my mind. It worked. My dick jumped. Valerie put a hand on my thigh.

"I thought we could have a day off," she said. "I thought I'd take you to lunch."

Under her direction, I drove west on Sunset through bleached-out Hollywood, with its whitish asphalt pavement and scorched buildings. And further west through the Strip, where it was still sweltering but at least business was booming, with guys dressed like I was today and chic young girls sitting out in sidewalk cafés where the temperature had to be 110. No Mexicans here, except rich ones and busboys; a different world from Silver Lake, the Junction, the Micheltorena Hill. Every sign here was in English.

We zoomed on all the way to the coast, then south to Ocean Park. I concentrated on driving, past crowds of pedestrians who didn't seem to be doing jack shit on a weekday, nothing, nothing at all.

"Turn here," Valerie said.

I did, and parked. We walked back up to Main. She stayed ahead of me and I watched her, a little squirt of a thing, elegant as hell.

"Here," she said. "I thought this might be fun."

Lula, a Mexican restaurant, with windows open to the sidewalk, painted in lemon, whole walls of lemon and bright green and tingling blue, but what made my stomach turn, made me know one more time I was a failure, were three or four giant paintings by Carlos Almaraz, some of his great freeway stuff. I had to remind myself Almaraz was dead by now, and it was pointless to envy a dead person. But here were more paintings, pieces by Frank Romero, huge graceful cars in motion.

Romero was only twenty years older than I was, maybe twenty-two years older. He had a big house and a bundle of money and a great rep.

I had nothing.

By now we were seated out in the courtyard, next to a wall of huge skeletons by Eloy Torrez, skeletons dancing, partying down.

"Don't look *that* way, look *this* way," Valerie said, so I sat next to her and looked out across a lemon-yellow courtyard banked by purple bougainvillea. The colors made me nuts. Here were a lot of upper-middle-class . . . *butt-fucks,* eating lunch surrounded by color, taking color as their own, their right, chomping down tacos, soaking this up as if they deserved it.

A couple of margaritas calmed me down.

"I love to come here," Valerie said. "This is how the world should be. Good food, drinks, windows open to the street. People having a good time. Not thinking! I even like the skeletons. They say Mexicans are in love with death. Why not? Better than fearing it, certainly."

"Yes, I will," I said. To my third margarita.

"The music, too," she said. "I love the music." She reached over, patted my upper arm. "I only came here once with my husband. He thought it was tasteless. But I came here with other people. Friends."

Was there something I should be asking her?

"Don't have a fourth one," she said. "I need you this afternoon." A better part of my mind began to register: yellow walls, that bright bougainvillea coming out of planters at the top. And the courtyard open to the sky.

We drove up the coast to Santa Monica. Again, she asked me to park and I did, out by the palisades. I saw the blue ocean and felt the sea breeze. Old men in white trousers walked through a green but mangy park along the top of the cliffs. Valerie jumped down from the van and I followed her across the street to another building painted in an alarming shade of yellow. The Hotel Oceana.

We went up the steps into a crashingly terrible lobby painted like one of the worst, last Picassos. Valerie leaned into a counter, checking in. "Le Clerc. Suite 314?" I thought, this is it, I'm a gigolo for sure.

The elevator opened on the third, top floor. We looked down into another courtyard, this one with a pool. Again, color smashed at us—mustard yellow? No, they'd oranged it down, but it was bright, way too bright. I followed Valerie to the room, where two yellow adirondack chairs flanked the doorway. She opened the door. I followed her in, and had to laugh.

More yellow! Just fucking bright yellow. And the bedroom was done in ink-blue wallpaper with two big white beds. And the bathroom was painted a clammy persimmon. Someone had gone nuts in this place. Or had a lot of fun.

She'd been here before, this morning. The second white bed had a white nightgown, white pajamas, a basket of fruit, some chilled champagne, some fresh herbs. For a second I thought *this is going to be too weird!* But I shuffled a little drunkenly up to her and planted a big kiss on the back of her neck. The years peeled back, or, more to the point, they didn't matter. I yanked off her cool linen and there she was in a lot of steel-gray satin and we thrashed around the bed, loud and athletic.

The first time was over and it was only three in the afternoon.

I wanted to do it again. Immediately. But she felt like a shower, just a shower, so I took one with her.

She cracked open the champagne and I sprawled out across the bed, drinking, feeling fine. I could do this forever. Make a living at it.

She closed the wooden slats on the windows. The second time

178 - Carolyn See

we did it in real deep gloom. I felt myself losing myself, I gave myself up to it, didn't think about it.

At six, she ordered up caviar from room service.

I stretched out on the bed and listened to her set up a little picnic in the living room.

Caviar. There were people in the world who did nothing else but this. Eat caviar. Drink champagne. She'd cracked the wooden slats again so that one wall of the suite opened up to outside light, and I saw that the yellow walls colored the air in here, made everything golden.

A couple of hours later, while the sun was still up, she opened the door and went boldly out to put her arms on the railings that marked off this curving third floor. I followed her in my pajamas. Three floors below us, the pool was empty, inviting and—to my eyes, anyway—sinister. You could cool off there, or die. The yellow building pressed around me, each story marked off by banks of purple petunia, blue lobelia. Down by the pool, someone had set up a buffet. Businesswomen in party dresses, the long flowered print skirts of Southern California, drank white wine and laughed.

At the other end, a grandma was having trouble with three little kids. "Careful! Be careful! Janet! Antoinette! Michael! You'll fall—"

Janet and Antoinette teetered safely along the side over to the lobby and the drinking businesswomen. Michael headed straight to the pool and plunged right in the deep end.

My whole body lurched. I climbed onto the railing, but Michael bounced right up to the surface and hauled himself out. His mother appeared and yanked him into the room. Hell was going to be raised. I felt queasy. I went back inside.

I told Valerie about it, about Tod, about Landry, about Millicent. About Angela.

We sat on the couch, holding hands. It was dark now.

"Valerie, this has been wonderful, you've been really wonderful . . ."

"I know we have to stop. You have to find your own life. But I wanted to give us this afternoon."

"What . . . will you do now?"

"Find out ways to be happy." She patted my arm. "*More* ways to be happy."

I didn't know what to say.

"I need to be of use," she said. "I suppose I'm sorry now I never had children. Wally and I thought mostly of ourselves."

"Wait a minute. Children? Are you telling me you like kids?"

"Yes, of course. How could I not?"

"I know a woman and some children who need you. I mean, they *need* you! But kids are messy. They're hard work. Can you deal with that?"

"Robert! What else am I supposed to do? Go on fucking and hosing until the grave?"

"Fucking and hosing? Did *you* say that?" I reached across the couch and grabbed her. For the last time.

"But remember," she said later in the dark, "I want you to remember about color. I never had enough of it, but you can have as much of it as you want. That's why I brought you to this silly, wonderful place. And don't mistake peace for happiness, as I did, for so long. Don't stay indoors, because time is so short, there's so much to see. And . . ."

"Don't worry. I'll remember all of it." A wave of what you'd have to call tenderness washed through me. I wanted to hold her and hold her, and not think about anything.

And I did.

C H A P T E R

18

On my last day—actually my eighth—as a present for Shelley, I got there early and brought Dave along to help. We were going to paint the girls' room and wanted to get done by noon. We moved beds around and laid drop cloths and I mixed up a pale yellow that—along with my flower pictures and those lavender spreads— made the space look like the inside of a really good Easter egg.

As we were cleaning up I got one of my ideas and checked with Shelley, who was out back watering the new flowers and playing with the kids. Would she like just one yellow wall in the living room, to pick up some sunlight in the morning? And maybe some whitewashed bookshelves, since I had those boards in my garage. Sure, she said, and Dave and I got busy with drop cloths all over again. We were finished by one in the afternoon. She gave us lunch. Dave could have gone home, but there didn't seem to be any point to that. We were all having a pretty good time.

"Would you guys like to stay for dinner? What if I made a couple of salads and some lemonade?"

She was looking great today, sleek as a seal, flushed and clean and happy. "Why don't I call that Valerie Le Clerc and see if she'd like to come over? I'd like the kids to know her better if she's really going to be taking care of them."

Yeah, sure, we said we'd like to stay. It wasn't as if we had anything better to do.

"But this doesn't mean I'm really going to do it, go back to school. I'm not promising anything!" For a big girl, she was acting downright kittenish.

Dave spent most of the afternoon putting up a swing for the girls in the backyard; I drove out for a few more pony packs of flowers. Valerie came over about five with a couple of bottles of wine and an apple tart. When Jennifer and Sophie saw her come in, they went straight for her legs and held on.

I kept thinking that this was my last day. I'd be coming back by, of course—Shelley and I were friends by now—but this was my last assignment in a professional capacity this summer. I took a lot of pride in what I'd done here. Shelley had her learner's permit to drive, her finances were in order, she was beginning classes on Monday at LACC, if she didn't change her mind, and the house looked great, considering. But mainly, Shelley herself was my big source of pride. All she'd needed was some friends. And a car. And a nice place to live. And a project. I had to think about it from an educated point of view. Could you really override a whole shitty life in just eight days? Maybe that was oversimplifying it. But what if it wasn't?

The afternoon turned into evening. It was hot, but not too hot, and we all took turns with the kids. We thought about eating outside but opened every window and the back door, and set a table in the living room instead. Things were looking good! I'd painted this table and these chairs a pale green last week; Valerie didn't have to worry, I was going ape-crazy with color here. I'd slapped a brush on everything that gave the least hint of being sad and gloomy. I'd surrounded this girl Shelley with the colors of what—bravery? I'd made it so she'd . . . have to be happy.

Because the thing about Shelley was that she didn't seem to have any yearnings to be someplace else. She didn't seem to be feeling all that bad about her husband; she took every little improvement or triumph as if it were winning the World Series or the Pulitzer Prize. I felt strange taking money for having fun hanging out with her. But when I remembered my first couple of days over here, I thought, yes, I deserved all the money, and probably a bonus.

Dave turned on a sprinkler, an old-fashioned one, in the backyard, and brought the girls in the house to get their hands washed. I set the table—was I going to turn out to be an interior decorator after all this?—playing around with yellow napkins against the green wood. Valerie went out back to get some mint to put in a vase—for the fragrance, she said. Then she and Shelley brought out bowls of tuna salad and spinach with olive oil and hard-boiled eggs. I put on a CD of Elvis Costello from my collection, another thing I'd added around here to cheer things up. Baby Spencer, who'd just started to walk, staggered from room to room playing peekaboo with anyone who'd go for it. I took a deep, appreciative breath. The place even smelled good, mint and fresh paint and food and flowers, a lot different from the stink I'd found when I'd come in eight days ago. We wandered around, getting set up at the table, and finally we were all sitting down except for Valerie—looking very nice tonight—who made one last run to the kitchen to bring out a plate of fresh fruit.

Then the front door opened and Sydney Ross walked in. It had to be him. He was a wiry man, you could see he worked out. He wore a shiny sports jacket, and looked straight at the floor. "We've got to get something straight!" he raved. "I left because I *had* to!

Life had become intolerable for me. My parents say I was irresponsible. Have you been talking to them? I forbid you to do it! *You* were the one who was irresponsible! I will *not* be railroaded into coming back. They can't make me do it. You can't make me do it. I'm still a young man. *No* one should be forced to live the way I was living."

"Sydney," Shelley breathed, and he looked up and took us all in. I could see that, for half a second, he thought he'd blundered into the wrong house.

"Sydney," she said again, and looked sick. "Would you like some dinner?"

"No. No thank you!" Still, he stood in the doorway, looking around. Valerie poured lemonade. You could hear ice cubes clinking in glasses. Elvis kept on singing. The kids looked at him. Sydney Ross narrowed his eyes. "What have you done to this place? Who are these people?"

"I'm the handyman," I said, in the loudest voice I could manage, "and this is Shelley's new baby-sitter."

"I'm just a friend," Dave said, waving affably. He was already sitting down, helping himself to the tuna.

Sydney got a look on his face and Shelley lowered her eyes. "I don't know about this. I don't know about this at all. I turn my back on you, and you fill the place with strangers!"

I kept on standing, kept my eyes on Shelley. She looked at me and took a deep breath. "They're not all strangers. What about the children? Don't you remember *them*?" She took a deep breath again, leaned back in her chair, and tried out a shaky grin. "Don't you? Sydney?"

"Well, goddamnit!"

He turned and slammed the door. And was out of there. We sat for a moment in stunned silence. Then Shelley squared her shoulders, gave a brave little smile, and said, "Well, what are you waiting for? Eat up!" After a little wave of nervous laughter, the rest of us began eating. The salads were great. Valerie's tart was terrific. And Shelley looked content.

After dinner, the women stuck the kids in the tub for their bath. Dave and I cleaned up in the kitchen. Valerie read the kids a story and said she'd be back on Monday for Shelley's first day at school. By then it was close to ten o'clock and she left.

Still, I hated to leave. My last day as a professional handyman, unless I got work on the weekend. The three of us watched a rerun of *Law and Order,* and after that I pulled myself to my feet. "Come on, Dave. We've got to give Shell a chance to get to sleep." But he didn't move. I sat back down again and we stayed on the couch as the eleven o'clock news came on, and went off.

"I guess I'm going to stay here for a while," Dave said.

Shelley grinned. A real grin this time.

"Oh," I said. "*Oh.* Well, OK. See you later."

Then I thought of wretched Sydney. "Well, *goddamnit,* Shelley," I said, "who *is* this man! Don't you think I deserve an explanation?"

19

But my handyman career wasn't over yet. Mrs. Landry called me Saturday morning to do some work. The arbor in their front yard had pulled away again from the front of the house. Ono thought it must have been because of a bumper crop of wisteria. I had a sneaking idea that I knew better. I'd heard the damn thing creaking and crunching as I'd done that Cyrano-Romeo thing at the beginning of the summer. Thank God, Millicent wasn't anywhere around this morning as Mrs. Landry walked me through it: "Ono didn't want to clip the vine until the last of the major growth was over, and I agree with him. But yesterday, you can see right here, he spent the whole day with it, and when he got finished, well, you can see, the arbor just pulled away from the wall, here, here, and over here."

We stood out in the front yard. Of all the neighborhoods I'd worked in this summer, I thought, Hancock Park didn't have it. The

186 - Carolyn See

money was here, but the imagination was somewhere else, above Los Feliz where the Walkers lived, or up in the Hollywood Hills where every steep slope hid either a shack or a palace, or even where we lived, where houses always gave you a surprise. Here, it was two stories and a lawn, two stories and a lawn, two stories and a lawn.

I was jealous, I knew that's what it was. I was poor, they were rich, something like that. No. I was furious that Angela Landry would sell out herself and her kid for two stories and a lawn.

"I don't know how you're going to fix it. The arbor is wood, the wall is stucco—I don't know."

"Is it OK if I sink a couple of four-by-fours, probably three of them, one on either side, one in the middle, up against the wall, paint them white to match the walls, then lay a one-by-four on top of them, flush with the wall, just under the lattice? I'd stay away from the roots of the vine, of course. But I'd sink the four-by-fours in cement. I'll take all day today to put in the first set, the vertical ones, then I'll come back tomorrow morning and finish the job in a couple of hours. Eighty to a hundred bucks, and money for materials."

I'm not very tall, but she looked up at me. It was hot this morning and she had little beginnings of sweat under her eyes and along her cheekbones. She looked tired. But who wouldn't in this weather? I hadn't seen her since the Walker party.

Then she'd called, with that talk about the arbor.

"What do you think, then?"

"I'm sorry?"

"I said, what if I give you a blank check for the lumberyard and you start right away? I'd like it to be done before Ono comes back on Monday. He says the whole arbor ought to go; it doesn't go with the rest of the landscaping."

"*He* doesn't live here, does he?"

"I don't want to argue with him. It's better to just get it done."

She was wearing one of her long dresses, but it was so hot—and
the humidity was so bad—that around her collarbones the cloth
stuck to her skin.

"Can I give you the check? Bob? And you'll have it done by tomorrow noon?"

"Sure. How's Millicent? How's . . . Tod?"

"Fine."

"OK. So, give me the check. I'll start right now."

It was so hot. Hard to get anything done.

But I took some measurements and drove to the lumberyard
and got the wood and a few bags of Redi-Crete and started work.
In design terms, Ono was right, I could see that. The arbor cut the
white front of the house in half. The wood looked dilapidated
against the stucco. It had been somebody's bad idea to plant wisteria here, but it wasn't my problem. All I had to do was fix it.

I took off my shirt, found a shovel and gloves, and started dig-
ging three holes against the front of the house. The holes had to be
fairly deep—about two feet. I tied a bandanna around my forehead
to keep the sweat out of my eyes and every push of the shovel made
me feel a little better.

Around 11:30, Mrs. Landry and Tod backed out of the driveway
to do some errands. It was the first time I'd seen him since the
party, but Tod remembered me. He leaned out the window and
waved. "Hi, *Bah*! Bah!"

I went over and grabbed his fist in my hand.

"Bah! Wanna play?"

"Later. When we come back," his mom said, and I went on with
what I was doing.

An hour or so later, another voice said, "Bob?" I turned around
to see Millicent and a couple of her friends in white shorts and
shirts, all part of one smothered giggle. I knew the friends must
know about me, and even though I felt like a fraud, I let them take
it all in, some California version of whatever that guy's name was,

Lady Chatterley's lover. The only reason I didn't hold my stomach in was that all the work I'd done this summer had trimmed every ounce of fat away. The cool handyman, for sure.

"How are you, girls?" I said, and wiped sweat off my forehead with the back of my hand.

"Oh . . . fine," Millicent said. She didn't even introduce her friends. "We're going upstairs now. Maybe we could go to a movie tonight?" She was talking to me. More giggling, from the girls.

"Well, OK," I said. "But I've got to get my work done now."

Every man should be a handyman. I'd never had a summer like this in my life.

I'd placed the vertical four-by-fours in their holes, poured the Redi-Crete by late afternoon, but the sun wouldn't be going down until eight or later, so I gave them a first coat of white paint. When Mrs. Landry came back, I said, "Millicent asked me out to the movies, is that OK with you?"

"I guess so. I guess it's all right. Be home by twelve, though. She wouldn't like me to say that, but be home by twelve."

When Tod came out in the front yard, I showed him what I'd done, then threw him up in the air a few dozen times. Millicent came out with those two nameless girls in tow, and said could we go see *Lone Star* at the Beverly Center? I'd be by at 7:15, I said, and packed up my van and left.

Back at the house, I played it for all it was worth.

"I need the bathroom, June. I've got a date. With a blonde. A young one! Of the opposite sex. You ought to try it some time."

"You plank," she said. "Go away."

"Even cretins get to have fun. How's *your* love life? Going out with that guy in the wheelchair who invented black holes?"

"Toad!"

I peered into the smelly gloom of Austen's room.

"I'm going out, Austen. On a date with a beautiful blonde."

"Grow up, Hampton."

Dave leaned back in his chair and gave me the answer I needed.

"How do you do it? It's been so long since I've had actual sex I don't even remember it. I might still be a virgin, I'll have to check the files. Although that might be changing soon."

"We're only going to a movie." But I didn't believe it and neither did Dave.

"Isn't she just a kid?"

"Yeah, yeah."

A nice kid. She was waiting outside when I came, and I was glad about that. A nice chat with Mr. Landry was not what I'd been looking forward to. She wore a white sundress with little straps. Her hair looked healthy and shiny, and she kept tossing it as we drove west to the Beverly Center, where the whole world seemed to be out, enjoying the last few nights of the summer, drinking cappuccinos, licking frozen yogurt.

"My last year was my hard year, because that was my junior year when you have to put in your first applications to college, and keep your grades up too, but I did it, and I applied to Harvard and Yale and Wesleyan and Brown, and Stanford, and, of course, Berkeley, but I really don't want to go there. We took one of those college trips back in April, Daddy and Angela and me. There was a terrible thunderstorm at Harvard. Angela liked Yale, but I really hated it. I won't get in there anyway, but I probably *will* get into Wesleyan, and probably into Brown. And this next year, this senior year, I'm only going to be taking drama and journalism, because I got everything else out of the way."

She paused for a breath and looked up at me. We strolled the third floor of the Center, waiting for the movie, checking everybody out.

"Daddy says kinesiology is nice. All of his best clients are always getting injured. But, naturally, he'd want me to do something he can relate to. Sports medicine. Or broadcasting. Or PR. Daddy really wants me to go to UCLA, but no way."

"Want to get away from home?"

"Not really. I *love* Tod! And Angela is nice."

During the movie, she put her hand on my knee. I kept my distance. We were in the real world now, the date world, and anything I tried would go down in real-world history. But it was nice, taking in a movie in high summer with a beautiful young blonde.

Afterward, she wanted ice cream. We sat at a little table with iron chairs. I watched her demolish mounds of it, bit by bit with her curling pink tongue, and then bat her lashes at me.

"You're bad!" I had to say. "You know it, too!"

"I'm playacting," she answered. "That's all."

At home, the first-floor lights were on. "Walk me to the door, give me a kiss good night, then go on up," she whispered. "I left the window open."

"Are you sure?"

"Sure!"

Why not? It was only playacting. We walked up the path to the front door, playacting. Millicent turned to me and said, "I really had a good time, Bob!" I said, "Me too, Millicent! I hope we can go out again sometime."

She said, "We'll see. I'm pretty busy getting ready for senior year. But you can call me."

I bent to give her a good-night kiss, and her tongue darted into my mouth like a minnow. My dick jolted against her and widened her eyes. "Night, now!"

I walked to the van, parked it a block away, walked back, remembered that first night, took a look at the house, realizing again that this was the last night of the summer, then shinnied up the arbor and into Millicent's room. She was waiting for me in one of her satin nightgowns. Playacting, but what a play!

I peeled off my clothes, grabbed my condoms, and leaped into her bed. Her skin felt like it did the first time, toned and buff and young. I began kissing her like crazy, really loving the look of her square white teeth in the moonlight, and the smooth blonde of her hair, and the dark of my arms against her white slippery satin. I was going too fast, but I had all night to make up for it.

"Millicent? Millicent? Have you seen . . . ?" The door opened. Mrs. Landry turned on the light, turned it right back off. "Oh. I'm sorry!" Closed the door. Her footsteps receded down the hall.

"It's OK. She won't tell. She's all right. Come on. It doesn't matter. She's OK."

Oh! I'm sorry.

I took a deep breath, let it out. Rolled over on my back. Looked at the ceiling.

"I'm going home now, Millie."

"You don't have to. Really."

"Yes, I do."

Sunday afternoon I stopped by Mrs. Walker's to say good-bye. Since the night of the big party, I hadn't been over once, but I couldn't go back to the Landrys' today, and I couldn't think of anywhere else to go on this last day before school started.

Starting back at school meant I could simplify my life. I'd be a student again. A student for as long as I could swing it. Then I'd find a . . . girl. Then I'd get a job. Work for the studios. Go back to advertising if I had to. Get a condo. (Just the word, *condo,* depressed me.) A condo. A girl. A job. I'd fake my way into the adult community. I'd live by the beach, maybe.

Something.

But first I had to simplify my life, because this summer had gotten out of control.

Before I went over, I stopped by the drugstore down at the Junction. The guy behind the counter saw me coming, and watched as

I unhooked a package of Trojans along with some LifeSavers, and put them on the counter.

"Why not buy them by the gross? You'd save a lot of time and money."

I pulled down two more rolls of LifeSavers.

"Suit yourself," the guy said.

I drove right past the Walker house, almost got lost way up in the hills, had to turn around and come back down. Then I almost drove past it all over again. The front yard fooled me. In the month or so since I'd been here, someone had been working on the lawn. It was deep, trimmed, velvety blue-green. Someone had been pouring on water with a heavy hand. The hedges around the front door looked so alive they seemed right on the edge of strolling over and saying hi. For the hell of it, I didn't go in the front way but went around out back. It was a warm day and there was a good chance of the family being out there.

I could see the turkey shed, and recognize my own painted animals still up in the trees. But the same vivid blue-green prevailed. She must have found a great gardener.

Mrs. Walker lay out in the sun on a chaise in a bikini, the backs of her hands spread out flat so that the sun could tan them to match the tint of her arms. God, how many times had I seen that in high school? Around the borders of the yard, three or four Asian guys in short-sleeved shirts puttered and clipped and trimmed.

I walked on over to her and she opened her eyes. Her fingernails and toenails were carefully done. She looked good. Better than I'd ever seen her.

"Oh!" she said. "Hi! Long time no see."

"I came over to say good-bye. I'm going back to school tomorrow. I won't be a handyman anymore."

She hitched her body up to a sitting position. "I got separated. Did you know that?"

"What happened?"

"It was right after the party. I threw him *out*, that's what happened. Michael hated the house and he didn't care about the kids, and he didn't like me. I couldn't stand him! He was a waste of my time."

She caught the eye of an Asian who was looking at her, and shook her head. *No, don't come over.*

"Did you know I have a sister? I don't think you ever met her. She lives in Calabasas, out in the West Valley, and you know how close we are here to the freeway. You can drive out to where she lives in twenty minutes. They put a new Gelson's in out there. Actually, it's a whole big building owned by Gelson's. It's a great place to shop when I'm visiting my sister. You know I'm not much the housewife."

"You're not so bad." I wondered where this was going.

"I like the kids and the animals, but I hate all the other parts. So, next to the Gelson's they have one of those Vietnamese nail places where everybody knows each other and you can get a manicure and a pedicure for twenty-five dollars and that includes the tip."

What did I care? But I had nothing better to do than listen to this.

"Besides women manicurists, they had guys. They had guys as well as women." She was looking at me intently. By now I'd sat down on the chaise next to her, my elbows on my knees.

"For ten dollars extra those guys would massage your legs for fifteen minutes, and everyone was buying that. Because none of us ever got that at home. They didn't look at the clock either. They're real human, Bob. They're very kind. They didn't count the minutes. Can you imagine? They all knew each other, and they talked in Vietnamese, all part of the same big family. There's a little girl who belongs to the owner, about the same age as Samantha. I knew you weren't coming over anymore."

"So?"

She gestured toward the guy trimming the hedge. "So, I met Tran. He speaks English and he's really nice. And his family loves my sister and me."

"He's a manicurist!"

"More of a pedicurist, actually. He's in great demand, but that's not the point. At some point I had to look at what was going on. There could be a cartoon—*What the heck is going on!* Mike had his girlfriends, that was OK. But who's going to come after a woman like me? In this city, I'm old. Well, *you* know. What was I supposed to do? Make do with a handyman and an iguana? I'm only thirty-nine. I've got to pay some kind of attention to my life."

"A handyman and an iguana! Who did you care about more?"

"You reminded me, you know. You reminded me life can be nice. But Tran needs me. It's different. It really is."

"What about the kids?" I was amazed at how pompous I sounded.

"I told you, they're a whole family out there. It's perfect for Hugh and Samantha. About a hundred cousins and uncles and aunts. I'm only beginning to figure them out. They're not failures, Bobby! They've got this great way of living. They all stay in a big house in Calabasas with a flat roof, and after dinner they go up there and sometimes they sing or somebody plays an instrument, and they drink iced coffee. They sit cross-legged and rub each other's shoulders. The women are so ladylike, but they seem very strong! They handle all the money. Sometimes we go downstairs to sleep but sometimes we all stay up there on the roof under the stars. And when they come over here—well, you can see what they do. They're very successful, Bob. They have a lot of money. They own a whole chain of nail stores. I think they're more successful than Michael. And the kids love them."

"But . . ."

"OK, *you tell me.* Tell me what I was supposed to do. Go on!"

"I . . ."

"Get a face-lift? Find some lawyer who's already dumped his own wife? Hope to God he can stand my kids? No thank you!"

"As long as you've thought this through."

"I have."

"Well. OK." I got to my feet. "I hope these guys are good with animals!"

Her face, which had been anxious, cleared. "Guess what Tran's bringing over as soon as he can find me a good one. A Vietnamese pig! They're very well behaved. And they love children."

I stopped at the first pay phone I could find on Vermont. "Hello, Ma? I want you to know I've been thinking about you a lot. I don't know what I can do for you. I really don't. But I'll try and come up with something. I'll do the best I can."

$\mathcal{E}$arly the next morning, I set up the ironing board and pressed my clothes. I stood in the middle of my room and checked it out again; made bed, half-empty bureau, clean little closet, canvases stacked against one wall, table next to the window with paints. A pretty thin life, but neat as hell.

I went on down the hall to the living room. No one home today. Dave was over at Shelley's. Austen was with Ben and Hank. June was at UCLA. The whole place looked pretty poor. I went over to the picture window and took a look out. It wasn't one of those days where you could see the ocean. Far from it. I looked down at the patio filled with weeds. Seventy years ago, when somebody first built this house, the city must have been a paradise, everything must have been new. This must have been a great place.

All I really wanted to do was to drive over to the Landry house, go on out to the backyard without checking in with anyone, start pruning and clipping and painting, feel the warmth of the sun on my back, and wait for Millicent or Angela or Tod to come on out. *Oh! I'm sorry.*

Of course, I could go and see how crazy Jamey and Hugh and Samantha were doing with that whole Vietnamese pedicuring army. The thought of it made me laugh.

My laugh sounded out in the empty house. Like I was a ghost. It was time to go.

I drove left on Sunset, dropped down to Wilshire, headed downtown. It was the last semester for Otis at this "dangerous" location, although I had trouble seeing what their real hang-up was. It was just LA. The school was close to an old municipal park, where the grass was worn right down to the dirt. I was early for class and walked around. Peddlers sold toys made from beer cans, planes and helicopters of snipped-up aluminum. I walked by the side of what used to be a pure, clean lake and what had more or less turned into a bog of garbage, old tires, paper, stuff that looked like seaweed, gallons and gallons of crap, except that the sun still lit up the surface of the water. The whole damn city was turning to shit. But what was I worried about? Who was I to complain? I'd had my chance at Paris and hadn't been able to cut it.

Two classes, one in life drawing, again. One in fundamentals of design, again. What was I even doing here? In the break between classes I stood out in the courtyard, scoping people out. Along with all the *other* people scoping people out. A mile from here, Frank Romero lived, painting those goofy cars, or elephants and stars, making thousands and thousands of dollars. Just up the street on Carondelet, Tony Hernandez, the photographer, lived with his novelist wife. Both of them were part of a legend of love here in LA. I was as far away from those guys as I'd ever been. Maybe more.

"Hey, Ace? Got a match?"

A husky guy with glasses looked past me, not at me at all, as he asked the question.

"Sorry. Don't smoke."

"No problem."

A young girl came up to me next, pale and freckled, with red hair parted in the middle and held on each side by green barrettes.

"Have you, did you come here before?"

"Excuse me?"

"I mean, is this your first year?"

"Yeah. What about you?"

"I graduated from Santa Clarita last June. I just moved into the city last week. It's big!"

Santa Clarita had to be a high school up north some place. The kid couldn't have been more than eighteen.

"You're living down here? This isn't a good place for a girl by herself. What do your parents say about it?"

"They want me home with them, but I told them an artist needs to be free."

She was so short I could see the part in her scalp, white and clean and perfectly drawn. I saw that she was shivering, and just when I was going to ask her if she was OK she took a breath and said, "My name's Barbara. What's yours?" I realized she was scared to death. Of me, of Otis, of everything.

"Bob. But you can call me Ace. That's what the guy over there called me a minute ago."

"I guess . . . class is about to start again." She'd spent all her social money on me and was heading straight into bankruptcy.

The afternoon class stretched from two to six, with a half-hour break. It was stuff I already knew, of course, but it was an easy way to spend time, with sun streaming in, and students alternately concentrating on their own work or moving around, looking at what other people were doing. Across the room, Barbara seemed to have made friends with the husky guy who'd called me Ace. I went over and took a look at her work. Very clean and neat.

Soon enough it was six o'clock. The end of my first day. I made a point of saying good-bye to Barbara and not telling her to be careful going home. It was broad daylight, and it was none of my business.

I decided to go for a walk before I went home myself, and headed up a side street, past house after house, little California bungalows painted Mexican colors now, vermilion, turquoise, lemon yellow, teal blue. All the windows and doors had been shut up with elaborate wrought-iron bars, and the little yards were either crammed with potted plants and honeysuckle and bougainvillea or left to go straight to hell, with dried-out ryegrass growing right up through creaky wooden porches.

What if you just looked at *this,* instead of going to Paris? What if you took this material, the way Carlos Almaraz took it before he died, took it upon yourself to see the magic in these little houses, with the freeway hanging in the sky like a big crescent moon? But how could you paint these big stout grannies that came huffing by without looking like some social-realist nut? And what about these gang kids, doing stuff like shopping for their folks now in the late afternoon, before they went out and killed people later? I thought again of Frank Romero and Tony Hernandez up in these scrubby hills, basically the same hills I was living in now, and how easily they'd found their material. Suppose I looked back to where I really came from? Uncle Bowlie and Uncle Hack with pink cheeks, striking match after match, or my mother in her dark apartment with ivy on that crappy wallpaper, wringing her hands and using up Kleenex. It was my stuff all right, but it was too damn depressing. *Hampton's Mother.* Christ.

I hit Wilshire again and headed back toward Otis. Down here, the buildings used to be fancy and fine. Now the upper stories held

God knows what and the lower ones had furniture stores with couches on the sidewalk. Here, on a corner, a woman stood with a galvanized tub and a dipper, ladling out soup to old Mexican guys who'd brought their own bowls and jars. It had to be menudo; I could see floating bits of tripe in there. She must cook this stuff at home, haul the whole thing down to the sidewalk, sell it off, and go home again. The men hardly talked to her. They paid her in small change, took their bowls, and ate standing up.

I walked on to La Fonda, the old Mexican nightclub across the street from Otis, doing a matinee show, probably for seniors. Over the years, it had become some kind of cultural monument. I heard the mariachi out here on the street, and stopped for a minute or two to listen to the music—pure happiness in the face of a reality that frankly didn't seem to me to be all that great. The afternoon sun tinted the windows of downtown LA a mile away a garish bosom pink. Amazing, what color did.

I turned at the corner and walked up the side street looking for my van. A new Range Rover rolled past with a squeal of brakes and tires. I automatically flinched. The Rover skidded just past me, the passenger door opened, and a girl flew out, head up, feet down, walking in air. The Rover roared on and the girl crumpled, covered with blood, right at my feet. It was Barbara, the girl from class.

Her face and eyes were sheeted with blood, I doubted if she could see. Her blouse was torn and her skirt was stained with blood. A few people on the street turned away. The matinee from La Fonda must have let out; those senior citizens, old women in lit-tle hats, began to cluster on the corner. Did I hear the Rover, coming around the block again?

"Hold on to me." I picked the girl up—she was so little—and trotted with her across the street to the door of La Fonda, where the hostess gave me a stricken look.

"She's been hurt. She needs help. She fell out of a car."

"She *fell*?"

"She got pushed. We need to get her off the street." I set her down on her feet. Her skinny little legs trembled and then her knees locked.

The woman nodded her head, took the girl by the hand, and pushed her through the crowd back into the dark club. I followed them. "I'll just be here at the bar," I said. I ordered a margarita and waited. After a while the hostess shepherded the girl back out, cleaned up and shivering.

"Who'd do this? It's disgusting."

I couldn't think of an answer and the hostess didn't really want one.

"Will you see that she gets home?"

"Sure."

The girl began to cry. Tears ran down her face and her shoulders shook. Behind her, a new crop of families in their party best filed in for the early dinner show.

"Do you want to sit here for a while, Barbara? Can you hear me? Do you want a drink?" But she was probably too young to drink.

"Can I have a glass of milk?" A nasty cut along her hairline still seeped blood; I could see that even in the dark bar. Her eyes were beginning to swell shut, her upper lip had been split.

"It's my fault," she said, "my fault. I'm so *stupid*."

"Who was that guy? The one who called me Ace?"

"Paul. You saw him today. In class."

"The big guy?"

"Yes." She picked up her glass of milk and drank, but her mouth was in such bad shape she couldn't wipe her lip. I took a napkin from the bar and carefully dabbed at it.

"He asked me if I'd like to go out for dinner and I said yes. I went home and changed and he came to pick me up. I climbed into the car, and—you know that thing in cars where the person driving can make the buttons go down?"

"Sure."

"He . . . he pushed *that,* so I couldn't get out, and then he began to hit me. Just like that."

"He didn't try . . ."

"No! Nothing like that. All he wanted to do was hit me. He was driving with his left hand and punching me with his right hand as hard as he could. He didn't say anything or *anything*! I'd try to pull up that little lock button and he'd push it down. But I undid my seat belt and I managed to open the door and then I guess I jumped out. Or maybe he pushed me." She began crying again. "But I want to know *why*? Why did he ask me out to dinner? And why did he get so mad?"

I had to walk her home. I mentioned my car but she said no thank you so quickly that I realized she was almost as afraid of me as she was of the guy who'd beat her up.

It was getting dark by now, and the cars and trucks that passed us had their headlights on. Every time a car passed she tried to hide herself behind me. I felt like hiding too. I didn't feel like I had the courage or the strength to take on an oversized homicidal maniac. And as soon as it was really dark the gangs would come out.

"Are you sure this is the best place for you to live? It's a pretty bad neighborhood. I told you this morning."

She was crying again. I could hear it in her voice even though I couldn't see her. "I have to walk to school. I don't own a car. And I can't afford bus fare. My parents said they'd give me one year of school, and that's all."

"But what are you going to do tonight? Somebody's got to take care of you!"

"I can take care of myself."

We got to a ratty three-story apartment building that looked a lot like the place where my mother lived. LA was full of these broken-down places. The path up to the main door was lined with rickety palm trees and dying cypress. A platoon of rapists could be hiding behind all that plant life, waiting for Barbara to come home alone. I could see she'd just now thought of it.

"Would you mind walking me up to my apartment? I could show it to you."

No security, no nothing.

She lived on the second floor, in one room that faced the street.

"See? I really liked it, for two reasons. One reason is the balcony"—a little fistful of wrought iron that any human would be a fool to step out on—"and the other is this. A Murphy bed."

She went to a side wall, opened a cupboard, and pulled down a bed that fell with an iron *clunk* to the floor.

"How old are you, Barbara?"

"Seventeen."

"Where do your parents live?"

"Santa Clarita. Didn't I tell you?"

"And they let you stay alone in a place like this?"

"It's a nice place!"

She sat down on the edge of the bed. I thought about it, and took the floor. There was only one chair, and it had some dishes on it. The only table I could see in the gathering dark was an upended milk crate. I glimpsed some art supplies over in a corner, and what looked like a stack of paperback books. No curtains. No shades.

"Should we turn on some lights?"

"It's too bright when I do. There's just that overhead thing."

"How long have you been here?"

"Since day before yesterday."

"And your parents just left you here?" I couldn't get over it. She was such a kid.

"They want me not to like it, so that I'll go back home. But I'm going to be an artist!"

"Why?"

"I—you should know why." She sat stiffly on the edge of the bed and looked right at me. "Because I want to see things other people can't see. Live in a world that's different from the one I grew up in."

"Shouldn't you go to a regular four-year school like UCLA? Live in a dorm? Make some regular friends?"

"And after four years, get married and have some kids and live like everyone else in the world? That's what I *don't* want to do."

She was too dumb even to know that women never made it in the art world. Especially out here. She sat there like an obstinate child, testing her split lip with her little finger.

"Can I go out and get you some aspirin? Do you have enough to eat? Anything for dinner tonight? Anything for breakfast?"

"I don't need anything. I'm fine. But don't leave yet."

Then I saw that she was shaking. The whole bed was shaking. I could see a piece of blanket hanging down, shaking.

"Could you stay here tonight?"

"*Me?*"

"Yes. You can lie right beside me. I don't think I can stay here alone. I was so scared last night and that was before anything even happened."

I shook my head.

"Please. Come and lie down with me."

I was the handyman, I was the fix-it man, I was the one who knew how to do it. But after this summer, I was tapped out. And I knew this wasn't something I could fix. "I'm sorry," I said. "I can't. I can't help you. I can come back tomorrow with some groceries, and I can give you rides to places, and I can put in a deadbolt for you, but, Barbara . . ."

She didn't say anything.

"I can't give you the real stuff, I can't take care of you—because I'm all out." I almost said, I'm too fucked up, but it would have sounded too dramatic.

206 - Carolyn See

"I'll come by tomorrow to see how you are. Or I'll send some-one. Something. You can put the chair under the door for now. You'll be OK. But I've got to leave now. I'm sorry." *I'm sorry.*

Which didn't leave me any better off when I got outside again. "You asshole," I whispered. "You stupid fuck."

And then I couldn't go home. It was like I didn't have one. *Duh!* I nearly said it out loud. *Tell* me about it, fuck face. I ran down the short list of places I might go—so short, now that I couldn't go to the Landrys'—and there was nowhere. I couldn't think of one place.

I started to walk up Carondelet because I couldn't just stand there on the sidewalk. I passed more houses, more barred win-dows, more families framed in yellow light.

Everyone has someone. Except me.

And Barbara, of course.

You could almost laugh.

If you could laugh.

I crossed Sunset, looking around at crowds of dangerous-looking gang bangers. Go ahead. Do it! You'd be doing me a favor.

But the guys who caught my eye looked away. Even they had to draw the line somewhere.

Above Sunset, I spotted the apartment house where Anthony Hernandez lived. I'd met Hernandez once at an opening. A big good-natured Latino guy. Making a living from his excellent art.

I walked up dozens of cement steps to the old-fashioned fa-çade, peered around the sides of the building until I found the name, pressed the doorbell. What the *hell* did I think I was doing?

Hernandez opened his door, looking puzzled. Behind him, lounging in a comfortable chair, was a beautiful woman in a black sweater and pants, holding a glass of red wine. Everyone had someone.

"You don't know me. We only met once. I'm Bob Hampton."

"I've seen you around. Come on in. Want some wine?"

"Thanks." He stood inside the door. It was a small room a lot like Barbara's. It dated straight back to the twenties.

Hernandez came back with wine. "Sit down, why don't you?"

"Bob Hampton," I said to the woman.

"I'm Judith."

Hernandez leaned back against the wall. "What can I do for you?"

"I started at Otis this morning—I already got a degree from UCLA. I went over to Paris earlier this year." I couldn't go on. I felt like a damn fool.

"What's the problem?"

I took a breath and found myself telling them. I was stalled, I didn't know what to paint, it seemed like I was trapped between the two worlds, absolutely unstuck from what people might think of as normal life, but completely locked out of that other, better world, you know, that one . . . The life of art. "Like what you have," I finished limply. What in the hell was I doing?

Hernandez and his wife looked at each other, didn't say anything.

"And I'm a . . . I'm a . . . I'm alone."

"What do you want, Bob?" The woman, asking.

"How? How did you do it? How did you manage it?"

"Tony always said he'd never get married, never have children. I'd done the other thing. Got married when I was sixteen and had a son right away. By the time I was thirty-five and came out here to LA, I was alone again. One night I went to an art opening where there was a band. This darling man came over and asked me to dance."

"I never dance," Hernandez said. "I thought I'd dance that night though."

"As soon as we started to dance, Tony began telling me he planned on devoting his life to his art, and that he absolutely never wanted children or a bourgeois life. That was his whole position."

"And she looked at me and said, 'I already *had* mine. What would I want more children for? I want to spend the rest of my life writing novels.'" Hernandez laughed. "That put a cramp in my style. But the more I danced with her, the more I thought this could be the woman I'd been looking for."

I looked at Judith. "What did you think?"

"He was a beautiful man. I was willing to go along with it."

I looked around the room. "But you both have talent," I said, cravenly. "That's a gift."

Hernandez went into the kitchen, came back with the wine. "We put in the time. You put in enough time, you get something back."

"Yes, but how do you . . ."

"What Tony is saying, you don't have to think *how*. You just have to do it."

"Yes, but . . ."

"Didn't you hear what I said? I went over and asked her to dance. I don't dance! But I danced when I had to. I danced for what I needed. So I got it."

The novelist looked a little troubled. "It's not necessarily easy," she said.

But her husband shook his head, shrugged away her objections, and spoke right to me. "Sure it is. It's easy as sin."

In the Landrys' backyard, on layered, blue, sealed cement, at the beginning of dawn, I began to paint a world seen through water. The world in a wave, a swirl, a pond, a pool. I could see shapes, I saw how they lost their edges but took on something else, a shimmer and light, a transparency. People as fish. Trees as seaweed. The world floated, the way Tod must have seen it. It looked *so good!* You could swim to it. Dive down. Let yourself glide up, held by water.

I knew what Tod had seen. Of course I knew! I was an artist. I'd hauled all my house paint, all my acrylics, over here in the dark and stacked them on the lawn behind me. I'd finish the picture I'd begun three months ago. The blue background was waiting. The scope, the space, was immense, with the pool at its center.

I began laying in the house, its inside, using wide, airy strokes, white stucco on the blue cement. I painted Tod's youth bed, the first thing I remembered, such a silly thing, but nice to have short bars around you, good to keep you from swimming too far. I painted other stuff, too, halls and stairs. I put this house in the back corner of the cement by the ivy, and went on from there. The house was open like the house at the bottom of an aquarium; you could swim in and out, go through walls, doors, windows. I put in gleaming shapes that hovered and darted and changed their minds. I painted a Conchitafish in a black dress with white organdy fins, eyes so big they held all of Mexico in them, all the earth floors, all the children and parents left behind, all the tears, all the endless sorrow of women, but still I had to make it so her rump looked funny, so solid. That fish hung attentive by the door and I realized the house was small. Just like the ones at the bottom of an aquarium, and there must be a bigger aquarium and another after that, and then lakes and then the ocean and the sky.

I stopped and thought about it, rocked back on my heels and looked straight up to the ink blue of the perfect, very early morning September sky. The moon, full and silver, still stayed high up, pale and clear. I thought it was time to paint in the moon, but it wasn't going to cooperate. Don't look to *me* for help, it said. Don't look up, look *down* for the answer, into the pool.

I painted in the pool, right by the pool. Oh! It was beautiful! I absolutely got it. The most beautiful thing I'd ever seen or thought about or imagined. It had to have a bottom, and I swirled in some Alhambra tiles, some Prado tiles, but remembered they had no edges, only light and shimmer. Then I waited, figuring out the rest of the picture, and I swirled the pool over with translucent blue green, swimming-pool green. But didn't it need lights? I dotted the sides of the pool with little brown paper sacks, each with candles in them. Earth, air, fire, water. I flicked in some sand beneath the candles.

I hit a narrow space here, four by twenty feet, and I didn't want to be an asshole but I had to tell the truth. I gave the whole space to Landry, horizontally floating, filling in everything, and made him look like a sculpin, but he'd *always* looked like a sculpin, that was the beauty of it—so ugly some people wouldn't even eat a sculpin if it was the last fish in the sea, but, *hey!* Was that the sculpin's fault? So I gave the sculpin's thin lips and flat face and pale eyes a look of injured indignation—Landry getting out of his Cadillac—that even Tod might see and figure out: I am the sculpin of all I survey, so shape up, ship out, do *something!* But he was so big, so full of himself, so caught in the margins of four by twenty feet that he couldn't turn around, turn the corner, he couldn't even get into the world he owned. He could only sit there and glower, poor guy, poor fish.

The sun cut the sky. A thin, thin slice, what was it, 5:30 in the morning by now? The moon had slid away. I stood up, arched my back, licked my dry lips. I moved my paints across to the big patch of cement on the side of the pool by the house; twenty by twenty-five feet, cluttered with lawn chairs, a table, an umbrella. I dragged all the furniture up onto the lawn. Reorganized my acrylics. Then I stood looking at my surface and you could say I prayed. How would Tod see Tod's World? From underwater. And everything would be true.

I started at the left, as you might see it looking down from Tod's window, with the billowy Millicent, all smiles and white satin, with willowy pink arms, pale, wet yellow hair, and bright open eyes, and teeth like mythic pearls. I made her a mermaid, had to, of course, and spent as much time as I could in this fast-moving dawn. I had plenty of cans of spray paint, silver and gold; I made her scales silver and blurred her sweet edges with lines of gold. She was full of energy and ready to move. And then, I had to do it, even though I'd covered her breasts with a lot of blonde curls, I dabbed a dab of pure silk pink right where those other lips would be, right there across her mermaid scales, and gave them a lopsided smile. *Babe!*

Over on the right, because life is grim, I splashed and sprayed a whole school of Landry acquaintances that I myself had never met, long and brown like smelt, poking in their sharp noses and bland eyes. Concerned without being concerned, curious about Tod, just nosing around. "Is there anything we can do? Be sure to tell us if there's anything we can do." *No,* there's nothing you can do! We could flick this water with our fingers and you'd all scoot away, but you'd be back.

I was painting. If I didn't watch out, I'd be bawling. No, I already was. I was laying my life on the line. What if I made a damn fool of myself?

I knew I already had.

But I knew I'd already found out something I could use later. Be sensible! Remember that I worked best on these big surfaces, that I'd always been able to work fast, and that all the information about suffering for your art was wrong. There was enough suffering out there, you were supposed to get rid of it. Because if we swim in suffering, there must be a way to break through the surface. Like a porpoise. Like a trout.

I sprayed a few careless bubbles up from the bottom and painted a watery surface, leaving plenty of room for brilliant air. I stood way back with spray cans in both hands, spraying lightly, laying down a light grid of gold and silver, creating air.

So what if I was grounded in tradition? There was a reason for tradition. And a reason women came up from the sea. I thought of Venus, and said forget it. I thought of the Virgin, no dice. I thought of another mermaid, no, no. So I did Tod first, a shadow just beneath the surface, carefree, a sea otter, floating on his back, playing, swimming backward. *Everything I see looks great to me!*

Was I going to have time for this?

Sure.

Of course.

Absolutely.

I inhaled all the air I could into my chest, and painted her in. Just the way she was. Walking on water. Wearing that brown and gold dress, her brown hair a little tangled, her face attentive but carefree. She was doing what she used to do, and must still do sometimes, looking into the water for an answer. There was her child, her sea otter. She knew him, but he was separate now. She gazed at him with endless love. Love and loss were the same thing and she knew it.

I sprayed bright gold around her edges. A halo. Why not? If anyone deserved it, she did.

And only now did it look like I might choke, or have my usual doubts. Because, get serious, had it ever worked out that when I said what I wanted, I got it? My father, lost and gone, told me, *forget it.* Quit while you're ahead. My mother, watching TV all alone, looked sad and said, *forget it.* Even sweet Kate, lolling in bed before she left to get married, heaved herself up on one elbow and whispered, kindly, forget it. Come on back to someone like me. Isn't it easier, just to have fun? And that twinkling mermaid I'd already painted in laughed unbelievingly. You have *got* to be kidding! Where is your *brain,* Bob?

I prayed. I really did this time. God, the Father, Son, Holy Ghost, this all goes out to you. This all goes up to you. This all goes up. Ask and you shall receive. Isn't that what you said? Ask. Ask. Ask. I'm asking.

For the first time in hours I had trouble with proportion, with perspective, with knowing where to start. Then I looked at her again, saw how her back was turned a little, and I painted in myself, right there, kneeling on the waves, just the way I was. I knelt behind her, to the side of her—I knew how I looked well enough, from long lonely nights looking in the bathroom mirror—I leaned my head in at her waist. Remembered not to stint on my own crinkly hair. Let my arms wrap loosely around her thighs. And in the picture, closed my eyes.

Because only I can love you. Because I know what it is to lose heart and still have to go on. I know what it is to be alive but glassed in, stuck in the aquarium. To be looked at but never seen. Sure, maybe later you'll meet someone, but what are you, thirty-five? You haven't met him yet, have you? Unless you look down, unless you feel this light touch on your legs. Could it be that you're not seeing either? That you think you're looking for the answers but you're not looking hard enough?

Because I haven't been looking very hard, not hard enough.

I didn't want to cheat, but I gave myself some great-looking eyelashes and realizing, thank God, that I hadn't dealt enough with her left arm, I let it hang down, relaxed, across my neck. Not a commitment, but a touch that might go either way.

Could *I* really stand it? Everything that this meant? Was I really in it for the long haul?

Sure. Because what else was there? Because you can't get a camel through a needle, or whatever that was. Because my life could be almost half over and I'd never loved anybody.

Or painted anything, until today.

And the small sour part of my mind that never really shut up suggested, at least after this you know you can paint murals on restaurant walls and make a decent living. Or banks. No nine-to-five advertising, ever, after this. No more classes, either.

But the rest of me was sanctified. I knew I'd done it.

I stood up and back for the last time—on this project—shielded my eyes with my palm and took a look.

Pretty good. The sun caught the gold paint and made the whole thing shine. But there was something else shining in there. I could see it. I knew it.

Now, I prayed again, *Do your stuff!*

I turned to the house. The sun was picking up, gathering strength, burning into my shoulders. Brushfire weather. Paint-drying weather. The sun made the house some fairy-tale fortress where the princess lived, and the dragon, and yeah, the queen, and a wounded prince. Come out, I said, and take a look at what I've done. I can't stay here too much longer or I'll pass out.

A door did open. Millicent, looking fresh as a soft-drink ad, her slim body sliding around under one of those nightgowns, took a look at me and then at my painting and then at me again. She opened her mouth and took a breath. I cut her off with a finger to my lips. She took my cue and kept quiet, but came closer. I watched her toes sink into the damp grass. She smiled at her dad, and her own outrageous mermaid self, then stared, perplexed, at her stepmom and Tod. And me. She turned to look at me and took a breath again.

But I shook my head. For once, I was going to have it my own way. *It's not for you. Don't you see who it's for?* Even as I did it, I said a regretful good-bye to her and all the girls like her, all the other girls and women who were still young and pretty and silly, all the girls I'd never have now. And good-bye to Kate and June and Jamey and Valerie, and all the accidental girls and women I'd ever had—quite a few of them. Because I wasn't going to be one of those Picasso guys. This was going to be *it,* as far as I could see. You could spend the first half of your life one way, and the second half another.

I ducked my head at Millicent, and pointed her back to the house. She took a last look at the family in the heart of my painting. It's your funeral, she shrugged silently, then gave me a sweet, affectionate, blinding grin. At least something's happening! Somebody had to do something, and you're the one who did it.

Yes, I am the one.

Then my heart began to pound as if it really were a madman in the cage of my ribs. Because the door opened again and she stood there, wearing the same brown and gold dress she'd been wearing the day when . . . Tod's life had changed, and my own life began.

Suddenly, I felt I might really faint, pass out, disgrace myself; my knees might buckle. I hadn't eaten in about twenty hours. Empty, empty. I had nothing left, well, hell, I never *did* have anything but this. Myself. I concentrated on standing up. Holding my ground.

She had Tod with her. He'd just woken up and stood rubbing his eyes.

She looked too, of course. She checked it out the way Millicent had, but quicker, more thoroughly. It burned her. I could see that.

Now it came down to it. I'd done all I could do. Played my last card.

She whispered, "Are you sure?"

She walked over to me. I could see the translucence of her skin, the few lines that hadn't been there three months ago. I could see her as a child, a girl, a woman, old woman. I loved everything I saw.

This time, her arms went around me gently, and the minute they did, I felt OK. The kid came over and leaned in beside us and that completed it. Her hair smelled of this morning's shower and her shampoo. "Are you sure?" She was saying it again.

"Yes, I'm sure." Then, it dawned on me where she was, holding on to me, and I laughed out loud. *"Yeah!"* She put her backyard whammy on me, the way she had that first day, cracking my neck with her muscular little arm. I had to pull back, just to see her face, and laugh.

Then Landry was out there. Without thinking about it, I did a melodramatic movie thing. I pushed her behind me and put out my right hand. "They belong with me," I told him. "After what happened, they belong with me."

Landry thought about it. He was probably fed up with the bunch of us. "I thought this was going on. I knew it! What do you expect me to do, *fight* you for them? They're both damaged goods, as far as I'm concerned." He curled his lip and shook his head, and went back into the house. Angela watched him go. I couldn't see what she thought.

We crossed the border the next afternoon and drove through Tijuana, across stone bridges to the sea, past the bullring with its flags blowing in the breeze. We headed south on the toll road. The ocean burned with blue.

We'd spent our first night in San Diego, in a big hotel room with two double beds looking out over Mission Bay. Ordered up hamburgers and big glasses of milk, the two of us watching television until Tod dropped off to sleep, then building a nest for him out of pillows on the far bed. We watched more TV, cautiously, like old married people, until the eleven o'clock news was done. We'd showered separately and she came to bed wearing one of my shirts. I'd had a speech ready about waiting until we could find the kid a separate room. I'd remembered the night with Millicent, how Angela had caught me red-handed. I thought that maybe the only thing in the world I really knew how to do besides painting, I wouldn't be able to do.

But I remembered again how she'd held me the day I saved Tod. I trusted her to do that again. I gave myself over to her, and she did. I lost track of all of it, I got lost in it. She's crazy about me, was the last thought I had.

Now it was afternoon again, past Tijuana, and we were into our second day together. The van hummed along the mostly deserted road, and the world sorted itself out into vivid color: white sand, black road, blue sky, blue sea. So beautiful!

We drove straight through Ensenada and turned right south of town, heading out to Estero Beach.

I'd never been there and it turned out neither had she. It was an old-time white guys' resort, with rows of stone-floored bunga-lows along a broad lagoon, and around the waters' bend, shiny lit-tle trailers that could have belonged to the Hampton clan, with retired Americans and barbecues and pet parrots and flags. We walked past all this after we checked in. The sun was setting. Then we walked back home, along the edge of the lagoon. Halfway back, I hunkered down next to Tod and said, "We've got to get something straight, buddy. I don't want you ever going in the water unless you've got your mother or me with you. We'll go with you whenever you want, but don't go in the water alone. OK?"

And Tod said OK.

We walked back over spiky grass, past vinca and birds-of-paradise into our cool room. Again, the world divided itself into big bright pictures, coruscating silver lagoon, silver-gold sand, sunset-pink sky. Angela walked up to the main building and came back holding a pitcher of margaritas, slushy with ice.

Our second night.

I wondered what she had planned for us, what *I* had planned, if there was a plan. But then I gave all that up, letting myself drown again. She was strong, and she was mad for me. I couldn't get over it. She whispered in my ear, "You do have skin like peaches."

Late that night, I saw her get up and move out to the stone ter-race. I followed her and we sat together, watching the moonlight on the lagoon.

"Angela . . ."

"Shhh."

"What are we going to do?"

"I've been thinking. For quite a while, actually. We keep on heading down the peninsula, down the rest of Baja. There's a little town just north of Cabo where they have a lot of American artists. You can work there. Start selling it."

I had a question to ask. "How long since, how long have you known . . . you liked me?"

"Since the first minute I saw you. Your hair! Your wonderful arms. The way you can't fix anything but you fixed everything. The way you are with Tod. The way you smell. Your wonderful skin. I thought I'd be too old for you, but I'm not. I'm not."

She reached across to me, grabbed my shoulders, pulled me down hard. We ended up stretched out on cool stone.

"Listen," she said, when we'd finished, and she sat on the terrace with her ankles crossed and told me a story about the life we'd have at the tip of Baja, living in a big house by the sea. I'd do pictures like the one I'd painted for her by the pool, and tourists would buy them for lots of money. I'd get a bald spot and a deep tan and wear turquoise jewelry. She'd wake up early every morning and go to the market for fresh vegetables and learn Spanish and drink hot chocolate with the Mexican wives and have some more kids. Tod would go to school and learn two languages instead of one. He'd skin-dive and maybe marry the mayor's daughter when the time came. Once a year, we'd all row out into the Sea of Cortés when the whales swam in to mate. We'd live together fifty years, and get brown and wrinkled, and Americans and Europeans would make special trips in four-wheel-drive vehicles to buy the original works of Robert Hampton.

I got up then and went over to the cooler where we'd stowed the second half of the pitcher of margaritas. The whole world seemed to crackle and glisten. I thought back to gray, cold days.

"You know, when I used to think about my future, I always figured it would be Paris."

"Oh, we can do that, if that's what you'd like, for a few months a year. As soon as you've got your reputation. London, too."

"I can paint you, to start with." My life shifted and creaked open again, like a rusty trunk with a hidden compartment, a second, secret cache of treasure. There was a whole world in there, another whole world.

"I can paint you to start with," I said again, taking it easy, or trying to. "I can paint you a thousand ways. I can start with that."

John Simon Guggenheim

Memorial Foundation

90 Park Avenue

New York, New York 10016

To Whom It May Concern:

May I request that the following note be added to my previous application of August 15 of this year.

<u>Re</u>: Robert Hampton

In searching out Los Testigos in Los Angeles, I would have been remiss had I not tried to discover the <u>Painting by the Pool</u>, the allegorical, hastily painted work said to have been created by the artist to win the heart of his wife, who was married to another at the time. The home is still owned by Augustus Landry, first husband of Angela Hampton and father of Millicent and Teodoro. Mr. Landry answered his own door, waved me on without a word out to the back, where the painting is said to have surrounded the swimming pool.

Nothing was there. I turned to ask Mr. Landry for an explanation, but he had gone inside, nor did he choose to answer my repeated knocking.

YOURS SINCERELY,

Peter Laue

PETER LAUE

Acknowledgments

I wish to thank the Getty Research Institute for a generous grant that included both the time to write this book and the institutional reassurance that great art may make its home in the west. I'm particularly indebted to Michael Roth and Sabine Schlosser for their kindness and to Charles Salas for his intellectual teasing and challenges.

For their insights into the mind of the aspiring fine artist, I'm grateful to Rae Lewis, Jo Anne Lopez, and dear Charles Buckley. My thanks and respect to Judith Freeman and Anthony Hernandez.

Special thanks to Ann Godoff, Lee Boudreaux, Jean-Isabel McNutt, and Robbin Schiff at Random House, Anne Sibbald at Janklow Nesbit, and Linda Kamberg de Martinez.

My deepest appreciation goes to my family, Lisa See and Dick Kendall, Alexander and Christopher Kendall, Clara Sturak and Chris Chandler. And of course to John Espey, my sweet love.

About the Author

CAROLYN SEE is the author of nine books. She is the Friday morning book reviewer for *The Washington Post* and has won both a Guggenheim and a Getty fellowship. She lives in Pacific Palisades, California, and currently teaches English at UCLA.

About the Type

This book was set in *Fairfield,* the first typeface from the hand of the distinguished American artist and engraver Rudolph Ruzicka (1883–1978). In its structure Fairfield displays the sober and sane qualities of the master craftsman whose talent has long been dedicated to clarity. It is this trait that accounts for the trim grace and vigor, the spirited design and sensitive balance, of this original typeface.

Rudolph Ruzicka was born in Bohemia and came to America in 1894. He set up his own shop, devoted to wood engraving and printing, in New York in 1913 after a varied career working as a wood engraver, in photoengraving and banknote printing plants, and as an art director and freelance artist. He designed and illustrated many books, and was the creator of a considerable list of individual prints—wood engravings, line engravings on copper, and aquatints.